TABOO

PENTHOUSE PLEASURES, BOOK 1

JAYNE RYLON   OPAL CAREW   AVERY ASTER

HAPPY ENDINGS PUBLISHING

Cover Art by Arijana Karčić

Editing by Mackenzie Walton

eBook & Print Formatting by Jayne Rylon

Version 2

Ebook ISBN: 978-1-941785-80-5

Print ISBN: 978-1-941785-81-2

One luxury building holds six penthouse apartments owned by kinky Manhattanites. Their sizzling stories will be told throughout the Penthouse Pleasures series from New York Times bestselling authors Opal Carew, Jayne Rylon, and Avery Aster.

From trailer trash to elite New York City lawyer, Casey Clark has transformed her life. There's only one change she regrets. The one that left her blazing her trail alone.

Her tough ex-boyfriend Jace West has made a career of protecting people in bad situations, just like he always did for her. When Casey finds something in her new penthouse apartment that could put her in danger, he's the first one to volunteer to keep her body safe—even if it puts their hearts at risk again.

Jace counts on his partner Ian to chaperone his alone time with Casey. Instead, it seems the guy balances out Jace's rough edges with a suave sophistication Casey always craved. The combination has the potential to fill the void in her life that money, power, and ambition can't...if she's bold enough to take what she wants from each of them.

Venturing into taboo territory, Casey could become the woman Jace has always needed. The kind who's enough for not just one super sexy man, but two of them.

ADDITIONAL INFORMATION

Sign up for the Naughty News for contests, release updates, news, appearance information, sneak peek excerpts, reading-themed apparel deals, and more. www.jaynerylon.com/newsletter

Shop for autographed books, reading-themed apparel, goodies, and more www.jaynerylon.com/shop

A complete list of Jayne's books can be found at www.jaynerylon.com/books

1

"Congratulations, you're officially the newest resident of Beekman Place. Welcome home, Ms. Clark." The cheery front desk manager plopped a set of golden keys in Casey's palm. Okay, so they probably weren't *really* gold, but gold-toned and shiny as fuck. They gleamed like everything else in the fancy lobby.

Major goal achieved. Hashtag success.

Casey officially lived in one of the most prestigious neighborhoods in Manhattan. Take that, humble beginnings.

After thanking the manager, she twirled her new keys around her index finger, careful not to mess up her perfect manicure as she headed for the private elevator that led to the penthouse apartments on the highest floor of the iconic building. The ride straight to the top in the polished car seemed surreal.

The woman reflected in the mirrors—with her stylish blonde hair, perfect makeup, and designer suit—was a far cry from the bedraggled white trash girl Casey had been before she'd known better. Only her wide, bright blue eyes seemed the same to her.

Could this really be her life?

Damn straight it was. Just because she'd grown up in a trailer park on the outskirts of some Podunk upstate town didn't mean she didn't belong here. After all, she'd spent the past twenty years busting her ass to make up for that inauspicious start.

She'd sacrificed everything for this.

Casey swallowed hard as she thought of her mom. Lorna had drank herself to death before Casey could afford the fees for a fancy rehab facility. Not that her mother would have agreed to go anyway. Then there was the one guy she'd pictured herself spending the rest of her life with.

She scrunched her eyes closed until the unwanted ghosts of loved ones lost dissolved.

A cheery *bing* announced her arrival at the top. Casey exited the elevator and crossed the wide hallway to her penthouse's door.

She aligned her freshly cut key with the lock. This was it. The moment she fulfilled the promise to her younger self about where she'd live when she grew up—a home without wheels, someplace classy. An apartment where she didn't have to lie awake at night wondering if one of the neighbors would bust through her window and hurt her. Or worse, if her own mother would sell her to them for a six-pack.

Her fingers shook as she slid it home and shoved open the door.

Head high, shoulders back, she marched inside the penthouse apartment.

Her penthouse apartment.

Sure, she'd only been able to afford it because the previous owner had vanished along with his long-overdue mortgage payments. The bank had been eager to cut her a deal on the place. Nobody had to know that, though.

Could that be why her victory seemed so hollow? Because it wasn't quite what it appeared?

Fuck that. It was still a huge accomplishment.

She hated the part of her that would never be satisfied, the side that constantly struggled to prove she was better than her roots. The piece that was a slave to ambition.

It wasn't that there was anything wrong with growing up in a trailer park. Not in and of itself. It was the specific bottom-of-the-barrel neighborhood and the defeatist mentality that her mother had reveled in that had been the problem. Casey couldn't stand the thought of succumbing to those innate tendencies. There had been plenty of times when she'd felt like giving up, slinking home, and learning to settle for something simple. Easy. A comfortable existence with the boy she'd fled from.

No. She refused to give in to the weakness she'd inherited.

Feet spread wide in five-inch spike heels, hands on hips, and shoulders back, Casey tossed her mane over her shoulder. She admired the city laid out before her like it was her domain. Hers for the taking. Except she'd already conquered it.

She'd graduated Columbia Law School in the top one percent of her class before a major venture capital firm recruited her to join their team as a corporate lawyer specializing in mergers and acquisitions. So far she'd been instrumental in seven takeovers and had even earned shares of the businesses she'd helped take over. Just last month, she'd been promoted to the head of her department when her mentor had retired.

It would have been easier to climb the outside of the sleek skyscraper she now called home. At times she felt like she'd clung to the path upward by her fingernails. But it had been worth it.

It was one of those moments—the defining sort—in a woman's life. Or it should have been.

Instead, Casey stood at the floor-to-ceiling windows, staring out onto the city far below her while wondering how she fit in. From way up here, everything seemed so distant, separate from the heights she'd struggled to elevate herself to.

Had she taken things too far?

Maybe there was more to life than work, promotions to more stressful positions, and ever-increasing bonuses. A fancy car, expensive meals at world-class restaurants, and even a luxurious penthouse apartment didn't mean as much if there wasn't anyone around to share her success with.

She wished her mom was here to see it, even if she would've been too drunk to understand the momentousness of the occasion.

A companion of the sexy male variety to share it with would be nice, too.

Casey promised herself she'd build an online dating profile and at least take a peek at a few eligible bachelors as soon as she'd finished unpacking and settling in. It could be fun to focus on finding a partner who could enjoy the perks of her newfound lifestyle. Someone to cheer her on and be proud of her accomplishments. Someone she could do the same for.

Otherwise, what was the point of having all this?

Getting laid couldn't hurt either. It'd been far too long since she'd had a decent orgasm provided by an actual man instead of a battery-operated boyfriend.

There she went thinking about the guy she'd left behind. Sure, he'd been gruff and immature, wild and crass. He'd also been gorgeous, and fucked like no one she'd been with since.

Casey rubbed her palm over her stomach, trying to squash out the emptiness there.

She nearly convinced herself it was simply hunger. After she'd finished devouring delivery from the top sushi joint in the city and the emptiness lingered, she knew it was something a lot harder to fix.

Well, shitcakes.

2

———

Casey set the last of her law books onto the mahogany built-ins of her home office, then stood back to evaluate her handiwork. Something about a third of the way down the shelf at knee-level seemed off. Her OCD tendencies kicked in. She knelt to rearrange knickknacks from her overseas travels when her knuckles caught on a ridge she hadn't noticed before.

Her hand jerked. She knocked over a goldfish figurine she'd picked up in the jade market in Hong Kong a few years ago when she'd done an independent study there on international law.

Shit! It hadn't been very expensive, but it was priceless to her. It reminded her of how aggressively she'd educated herself—eradicating her ignorance about the world and all the possibilities it held both through formal schooling and by seeking out new life experiences—after fleeing from home.

It also reminded her of the young badass who'd once shown her a glimpse of his softer side when he won her a fish at the county fair. He'd also helped her repair a cracked aquarium that had been sitting in an abandoned lot they walked past on the way to school, and rummaged an air pump from a garage sale so her pet was taken care of. Though it wasn't a kitten or a puppy like she'd dreamed of, it had kept her company and given her someone to talk to on the nights she found herself alone, afraid her mother might not make it home after last call.

The stony fish bounced off the inside edge of the bookcase then clattered to the shelf, seemingly unharmed. *Whew*!

When she reached in to right it and check for chips, a panel in the back of the bookcase popped out. "What the—"

Casey pried it open. Behind the secret section was a steel door, complete with a dial and a handle.

A safe.

That made sense, she supposed. Anyone who could afford to live here would likely have valuables to secure. Even she had a few nice pieces of jewelry she wouldn't mind tucking away, and she was almost certainly the riffraff in this neighborhood.

She'd tried not to let the mystery of the previous owner's disappearance color her feelings about the penthouse apartment she'd snagged at auction. Other people had obviously been turned off by the potential bad luck that could befall someone living in a place a man had disappeared from. It was the only thing that could explain how she'd practically stolen this apartment.

With a shrug, she tugged on the handle. Unsurprisingly, it didn't budge.

Casey took out her cell and tapped the contact for Everly Wright, the building manager.

The chipper woman answered in less than three seconds. "Good morning, Ms. Clark. How can I help you?"

"Hey, Everly. I was wondering if you have the combination to the safe in my library. Is there some default code I need to enter before I can reset it?"

"Oh. Um. No. I mean, I double-checked the files before you moved in, when I was compiling the folder of reference information." The usually unflustered woman hesitated. "There is no record of a safe we installed in that apartment. It must have been added by the previous owner after closing."

Casey had probably read a few too many battered Nancy Drew books from the mobile library van that had been the highlight of her summer days as a kid. In addition to sparking her interest in the law and discovering the truth, they had instilled her with an obsession with puzzling situations that piqued her curiosity now. Besides, her contract on this place had included a few unusual terms due to the absent previous owner. For example, she'd agreed to accept everything in the apartment as part of the transaction.

Of course, that had saved the bank some money cleaning the place out, and had spared her the hassle of buying new furniture. What if there was something valuable in the safe? Or a clue as to where the preceding resident had wound up?

It would rightfully belong to her.

This was even better than taking a box of junk on *Antiques Roadshow* and finding out you'd been living with a Fabergé egg in the attic. Kind of.

"Could you put me in touch with the locksmith you use for the building?" Casey asked.

"Absolutely." Everly chuckled then. "I hope you don't mind me saying, I'm dying to know what's in there."

"You and me both." Casey grinned. "I'll keep you in the loop. Or you can come up with the locksmith if you'd like to see for yourself."

"If you don't mind, I think I will."

"Maybe I should make some popcorn. I don't have any beer or wine here yet." And never will, she added silently. "But I've got some pretty fabulous herbal teas if you'd like a cup while we wait. It's the most excitement I'm likely to have this weekend."

"You and me both," Everly grumbled, then cleared her throat, attempting to maintain her cloak of professionalism. "Thank you, but I need to finish some things here in the office. I'll buzz you when the locksmith arrives, Ms. Clark."

Casey hoped she could start her transformation from a woman on a professional mission to someone who knew how to make friends with Everly and socialize again. She could relate to the woman, who was young and driven, obviously working her ass off to climb the hospitality ladder. Maybe they could go out for dinner or to a yoga class or catch a show sometime.

"Please, just call me Casey. Offer the guy double if he hustles, would you?"

"You got it. Thanks." Everly disconnected.

Casey ran her fingers over the sealed safe. Sometimes things were better left uncracked. If you knew what was inside them, it might not be what you had hoped for.

She'd learned that lesson the hard way.

For the third time in a single day, she thought of Jason West. Sometimes she went months without him crossing her mind. Others times, like now, she fixated on what he would think of the woman she'd become.

Would he approve? Or would he despise the new, stronger, independent version of the girl he'd tried to shelter from the world, including his own secrets?

It'd be unfair of him to judge, considering how much of himself he'd hidden from her. While pretending to be the romantic guy who won his girlfriend a goldfish, all along he'd been concealing his deepest desires. Taboo lusts that had simultaneously freaked her the fuck out and made her curious when she'd heard rumors of what he really liked.

After a lifetime of being known as the daughter of the town drunk, Casey hadn't been willing to risk another label. One a lot more damning, which would give the gossips enough ammunition to take down her fledgling career.

Besides that, he'd shattered her trust. He'd been the only person she leaned on with no reservations. Yet when she'd confronted him about what she'd heard, he had neither confirmed nor denied it. He hadn't come clean with her. She could see it in his eyes.

His betrayal had ripped her open. It hurt worse than the perpetual disappointment she'd suffered with her mom. At least she expected that.

So she'd run.

And he'd let her go.

Casey shook her head and concentrated on what had to be done next. It was how she'd survived those first indescribably painful months on her own and all the years that followed. If she was having trouble maintaining her edge lately, it was only because she'd checked so many of her goals off her list. Here she was, at the top and floundering.

She needed to sit down and map out what she wanted to strive for next to keep her thoughts from wandering to unproductive places. Soon. As soon as she found out what was lurking behind her bookcase.

3

A few hours later, Casey crouched beside the locksmith, peering over his shoulder.

The door to the safe swung open.

Even from where she stood, with him partially obscuring the interior of the small secure space, it was pretty obvious there were no giant diamonds or fat stacks of cash inside. Damn.

"Well, shit. That's a letdown, huh?" The guy deflated, his bulky shoulders sagging. He hitched his pants up, thankfully covering his kind-of-hairy crack—not that she'd intentionally looked—then shuffled aside. "I was rooting for treasure. Instead it's only some dumb papers."

Casey sighed and reached inside, expecting to find the usual. A birth certificate or a title to a car, something like that. Instead, when she withdrew a plain manila folder and set it on her desk, she was surprised to discover diagrams inside.

It took her a second to figure it out. Not Everly. Familiar with the area depicted, the building manager cursed immediately without even trying to obscure the f-word under her breath. "Why are those in there?"

Those would be blueprints of the six penthouse apartments in this exact building, along with copious notes on each. Casey deduced that was what they were because the paper on top was a depiction of her own penthouse. It marked a section of the bedroom closet with a green square. An arrow led off the page toward the unit next door.

On the second page, the arrow continued along the back wall of the second apartment, until it reached a spot somewhere in the ceiling of her neighbor's guest bathroom.

Below the green line were neat bullet points.

- *Leaves between five and six on weekday mornings to meditate in the park.*
- *Volunteers at South Street Food Pantry, Homeless Shelter, and/or the Manhattan Furniture Bank every day.*
- *Dog left home, crated. Friendly.*
- *Wealth inherited from elderly friend/parishioner.*
- *Occupation: Ex-priest. Philanthropist.*
- *Returns no earlier than five on weekday evenings.*
- *Items of interest: gold reliquary containing first-class relic of St. Francis of Assisi, antique Bibles, diamond cross, religious paintings by world-class artists including Rembrandt, Diego Velázquez, Salvador Dalí, and Raphael.*

"Holy shit." Casey thumbed through the remaining pages. Six in all. Each was more detailed than the last. They included more info on her neighbors than she was comfortable reading. Something sketchy was going on here. Or *had* gone on.

She handed the papers to Everly, who repeated her motions. The woman's face turned ashen before she whispered, "Those green lines. They're running along a channel that allows for utilities—wiring and pipes and stuff—to pass from unit to unit up here."

"You think the guy who lived here was planning to go for a little tour of the penthouses?" Casey didn't need the other woman to agree. She was sure of it.

Everly nodded before handing the documents back to Casey. "You're a lawyer, right? I'm probably going to need copies of those at some point."

Casey agreed then tucked them neatly into the folder. The locksmith looked down at the file shaking in her hands, then up at her with a bigger frown than before. "I think you'd better call the cops."

Fuck her life. She knew what would happen if she did.

There was no other option, though.

What if the guy who'd lived here before hadn't run off with his young, busty lover to some remote tropical island with a tax-dodging offshore account as they'd suspected? What if he'd been caught doing something like this somewhere else? Or worse...what if the man had been innocent and dispatched by whomever had placed this dossier in her safe while taking advantage of the vacant penthouse for the past year or so?

They might not take kindly to her booting them onto the street or foiling their heist plans.

"I think you're right." Casey shivered and plopped into the expensive leather chair behind the ornate desk. She buried her face in her hands. Because Jace West was about to get an impromptu tour of her new home.

It didn't matter how big the city was or what his official position was on the police force. She'd found out he belonged to it when she'd stalked him on social media during a weak and lonely moment a while ago. If Jace heard she was in trouble, he'd be there.

Why didn't that thought bother her as much as it should?

Casey braced herself, then searched for the non-emergency number for the NYPD.

4

It took even less time than Casey thought for Jace to materialize on her brand-new doorstep. Within a half hour, he had arrived at the scene and started demanding answers to a rapid-fire barrage of questions. She heard his husky voice, and a smoother one telling him to settle down, before she saw him.

When she rounded the corner from the living room, he was about to plow past the bellman, Lenny, and the first responders who'd been milling about in the entryway for a while now, waiting for two hotshot detectives. Casey hadn't even bothered asking for their names. Her gut told her it would be him.

That didn't mean it was any less of a shock to her system when her hunch became reality.

The familiar yet deepened timber that issued commands set her at attention. He used to bark orders at her like that in bed right before he slapped her ass and plunged his cock into her very willing body. She hoped her hard nipples weren't showing through her thin lace bra and silky handkerchief top when she faced the love of her life in person for the first time in a decade.

She barely resisted the urge to fluff her hair or strike a flattering pose when his laser-beam stare locked on to her, warming her from the inside out.

Worse, he was wearing jeans and a charcoal sport coat over a tight-fitting navy knit shirt. A damn sexy pair of jeans that flattered his oh-so-grownup and fleshed out body. He obviously hadn't kicked his running habit and probably expanded on it with some serious weight training at the gym. *Damn.* It was a hell of a different look for him than the holey sweats from the secondhand store. He'd practically lived in those as a kid.

You know how most people take an extremely flattering picture of themselves, apply filters until it barely resembles reality, and then use it as their icon for online profiles? Not Jace. He was even more attractive in person than he'd been in the snapshots she'd spied after a mutual friend had tagged them both in a ridiculous meme about growing up dirt poor.

Casey had deleted that fucker ASAP. Hopefully before her co-workers had seen it. Then she'd snooped around in his profile. She wasn't proud of it, but she hadn't been able to look away. Jace had always been handsome. Now he was devastating. Especially since she'd noticed his relationship status: single.

She fingered the jade figurine she'd stuck in her pocket after calling the police. Rubbing the smooth stone repeatedly had soothed her as she waited for the inevitable. It also gave her hands something to do right then. Otherwise she might be in danger of sprinting toward Jace, flinging herself into his arms, wrapping her thighs around his trim hips, and burying her fingers in his thick, dark hair or dragging them over his chest to see if it was as chiseled beneath that soft, stretchy fabric as she anticipated.

He'd been the hottest guy in her town when he'd taken her virginity. No one she'd been with since had come close to exciting her like he had either. How much pleasure would he be capable of giving her with an extra decade of experience under his belt?

"Casey." Why? Why did he have to say her name like *that*? Like he wouldn't be opposed to ripping her clothes off and showing her precisely how much he'd matured since they'd slummed it together, right there on the spot, onlookers be damned. She nearly choked.

"Detective West." Oops. She hadn't meant for his name to sound so sultry. Her throat was tight and her mouth had gone dry, though. So she accompanied the breathy greeting with a brusque nod. He didn't have to know that using his title had her squirming inside, instantly and uncomfortably aroused. She did her best to avoid dropping her stare to the handcuffs on his belt or the spot where the denim hugged his package, highlighting the portion of his anatomy she would most love to become reacquainted with. If only things were that simple.

"Oh, come on." He scowled at her.

"Just keeping it professional." She shrugged one shoulder, noting how his gaze lingered on her bare skin. Damn tank top. She hadn't been expecting company when she'd picked her outfit this morning.

The second detective, whom she'd already forgotten about, slid between them. He acted as the buffer they both needed to keep their reunion from deteriorating into either an epic fight or an epic fuck right there on her marble floor.

"Ms. Clark, I'm Detective Ian Ross. We're partners." He gestured to Jace with a single jack of his thumb over his shoulder. Where Jace was rough and forceful, his partner was smooth and charismatic. The ultimate good cop.

Partners, huh? Ian seemed more like a chaperone. The Hyde to Jace's Jekyll.

"Thank you for coming." She extended her hand and he shook it. Firmly enough to acknowledge her own strength, yet not so hard that it seemed as if he was trying to prove how big his dick was, like some of the arrogant bastards she interacted with at work.

"Are you okay?" Jace stepped forward, reaching out as casually as he had the nine million other times he'd touched her. He brushed her hair away from her neck and rubbed the pad of his thumb over her cheek as he had every time he'd promised her things would be okay. That they were only going to get better from then on out. He'd been right. Except she'd always imagined they'd be improving their lives together, not separately.

Casey hadn't prepared herself for such intimacy. She hadn't hardened herself against the effects of his tenderness. Her eyes drifted partway closed as she leaned into the caress. It felt so familiar. She'd missed his bold displays of affection.

Son of a bitch.

She shook him off and stepped backward.

"I'm fine." She crossed her arms, hopefully obscuring the betrayal of her body at the barest of contact with Jace —and his partner, for that matter. For a moment, she'd been connected to them both simultaneously. It would have been impossible not to imagine a scenario where their innocent contact became something far more inflammatory, considering her history with Jace and the reason they'd broken up.

"I think that's an understatement," Ian said softly.

Casey thought it might have been sexual innuendo until she realized he was looking beyond her to the luxurious apartment and the urban landscape stretched outside her windows. When she relaxed, his eyes shifted and he swept his gaze over her, making it clear his comment hadn't been quite as innocent as he'd probably like her to think.

She had to get this done with and send the pair of steamy detectives on their way before things spiraled out of control. Forget that dating site she'd been thinking of yesterday, too. After spending time in the presence of these men—smelling them, experiencing the instant sexual tension crackling through the air between them—no one would live up to this standard. Jace was her ultimate fantasy, and his partner wasn't shabby either.

Ian possessed a calming vibe that helped ground her despite Jace's nearness. A trait she very much appreciated right then.

Jace turned to the two uniformed police officers and Lenny. "We'll take it from here, guys. Make sure the two of you leave via the service entrance. Don't draw any more attention to the situation than necessary until we figure out exactly what's happening here."

The cops nodded and tipped their hats before escorting Lenny back to the lobby.

Jace crowded Casey, nudging her toward his partner. Trapped between them, she suddenly couldn't think of anything except what that might feel like under different, much more pleasurable, circumstances.

Everly cleared her throat from the kitchen. The open-concept floor plan made it easy for her to see exactly what was going on. From the raised brow she winged in Casey's direction, she saw a little too much. More than Casey intended.

Casey extricated herself from their grasp and headed toward the other woman. "Detectives, this is the building's manager, Everly Wright."

The guys advanced deeper into her home, making her wonder if she'd ever get the sight of Jace and his partner filling the place with their powerful presence out of her brain. Fuck them. It would always feel empty after they'd gone.

Jace rested his hand on her lower back, in the dip of her spine. It seemed natural. She'd missed the weight of his palm there and the heat that flowed through his fingers, threatening to scorch her.

It was right about then that she realized there was no way he was going to leave here, tonight or some other time, without giving her a do-over. There was too much energy zinging between them to leave it unexplored. As adults, would they be better at corralling that reckless passion? Indulging their physical magnetism without involving their hearts?

Ian looked over at them and shook his head slightly.

To her, the gesture didn't seem disapproving. More like an "I told you so" aimed at Jace or a "this should be interesting" mental note to himself.

Casey figured it would be hard to deceive a detective, or two, so she didn't bother trying.

It was no secret she lusted after Jace. Always had.

They were consenting adults. If they wanted to have a reunion fling, so be it. If they reveled in their effect on each other for the five or ten minutes it would take for her to file a report then move on with their lives, at least she'd gotten to see him again. Happiness swept some of the gloom from the situation as she realized he wasn't only surviving, but thriving. That's what she'd always hoped for him.

Despite the smoldering attraction that threatened to turn her new penthouse into cinders, Jace and Ian snapped to attention the moment Everly and Casey began to explain the situation and what had led to their call for assistance.

They pored over the file before Jace lifted his gaze to hers. "We've been investigating the disappearance for ten months. When I saw your name come through on the new title, I almost died. I was planning to stop by in a few days, to ask some questions...and see how you're doing. I'm relieved you're bringing this to our attention before we discovered it ourselves, but pissed that now you're involved. This is dangerous business. I don't want you anywhere near it."

"Seriously?" What were the odds of that? Casey didn't believe in fate or luck. Maybe it wasn't too late to start. "I assumed you were being your usual overbearing self by showing up here tonight."

"So you do know each other..." Everly squinted at them.

"Yeah." Jace scrunched his eyes and pinched his nose between his thumb and forefinger. "To you both."

Ian explained for Everly. "They were high school sweethearts."

Funny, that's not at all how Casey would categorize their relationship. It was so much more than that. Deeper, more meaningful. Soul-crushing when it ended. The twist to Jace's sexy lips made her think he agreed with that, at least.

Everly was smart enough, and tactful enough, to drop the subject.

Casey shifted their attention back to the important stuff. "So what do you know and do these papers help your case?"

"Off the record, we suspect that the previous owner of this apartment was a high-class thief. An enterprising up-and-comer who started cutting his boss out of the picture and taking jobs, for full price, on his own. He was careful. No one knew he lived here under an assumed name. This was both a hideout and, from the looks of these documents, a way to break free for good. An early retirement plan, I guess you could say." Jace paused then and looked at Ian.

"Well, we already knew he took off, right?" Everly bitched, "This place has been vacant for nearly a year. It's been a giant pain in the ass to work through all the red tape with the mortgage company and lenders to get it on the market again. It doesn't look good for us, having an open spot for so long. Being sold out makes the apartments downstairs easier to turn over. Demand creates demand. No offense, Casey, but the average home value took a huge hit when they let this place go cheap."

Jace shook his head. "That explanation doesn't ring true to me. This guy was meticulous. If he'd really gone off the grid, he wouldn't have done it in a messy way that left unanswered questions. Leaving something like this behind that could trip him up later? No way. My guess is that someone caught on and made an example of him. But we don't have enough proof of that to take down the ringleader."

Ian grunted as if he disagreed.

"This file really does lend a lot of weight to Ian's theory. One he's been trying to convince me of for a while." Jace clapped him on the shoulder. "Looks like you're going to win that bet, buddy."

"I'll let you know when I'm ready to claim my prize." The curl of Ian's lopsided smile made Casey tingle, though she wasn't quite sure why.

They might have had a lot more to say about the situation, except right then Everly's phone started buzzing, flashing, and ringing all at once. She frowned and glanced at it. "Oh shit."

Ian leaned toward her and read the messages pouring onto her screen. "Son of a bitch! He's not that stupid, is he?"

"I'm going to shut it down, I'm sorry," Everly called over her shoulder as she dashed out the door.

"What?" Casey asked.

Jace looked to Ian, who jogged over to her TV and flipped it on. The usual afternoon programming had been interrupted for breaking news. And there was their friendly neighborhood locksmith, blabbing to the media about what they'd found, the missing previous owner, and his wild speculations about what was going on.

As they watched, Everly burst onto the scene. Smoothly and efficiently, she requested that the reporters leave their private property while leveling an icy glare at the locksmith, who'd never work in her building again. Casey was sure of it.

Unfortunately, the damage had already been done.

Ian clicked off the screen and dropped the remote onto the couch. He ambled back to them before addressing Jace. "You going to break it to her or will it be better coming from me?"

Casey flicked her stare between the two cops. She didn't like the sound of that.

"Now that your locksmith got his fifteen minutes of fame, I don't think it's wise for you to stay here alone in case one of two things happens." Jace sighed. "Either the guy who exterminated our resident thief will come to check the place out and hunt for valuables and additional incriminating evidence or—if he's less dead than we suspect—the original owner could make a reappearance and be none too happy about you exposing his plans."

She rolled her eyes, unsure it was necessary for her to abandon her new home for who-knew-how-long when all she wanted to do was finish unpacking then fall asleep in her own bed. Then again, she'd never known Jace to be melodramatic...except when it came to her safety.

His overprotective streak had largely caused the rift between them, hadn't it?

"Do you agree with him, Ian?" she asked, counting on him to be the voice of reason. It was weird having a third person as a sounding board to keep her and Jace in check. When emotions ran as high as they did between the two of them, sparks—of passion or anger—often flew.

Their inability to stay calm around each other had contributed to the demise of their relationship. It was impossible to communicate effectively when you were either screaming or having raunchy make-up sex constantly.

"I do." He smiled softly at her, making her sure she was going to hate the rest of what he had to say. "I honestly believe there are people who will want insurance against any other damning info coming to light."

"So either you're going—which I would prefer—or, at the very least, we're staying." Jace crossed his arms and spread his legs. He seemed as immovable as the Statue of Liberty. There was no way she'd budge him. Honestly, she didn't even want to try.

Mostly because she wasn't crazy enough to relish the thought of facing a murdering career criminal or a disgruntled burglar on her own. She'd be lying if she said the thought of having an excuse to keep Jace close for a little while, especially under the watchful eye of his partner, didn't tempt her. Thrill her, really.

"Better have someone pack you guys an overnight bag then." She shrugged, as if it meant nothing to her to have them invading her brand-new territory.

"Babe, you know I sleep naked." Jace grinned impishly, then shocked her by sneaking in a quick kiss on her cheek. "Feel free to barge in without knocking."

Some things never changed.

5

———

"Can I talk to you outside for a moment?" Casey could have invited Jace into her bedroom for a private chat, but that would have been a colossal mistake. They'd never be able to have a rational discussion within reach of a bed. It might have been years since they'd spoken, but their chemistry was as instant and intense as ever.

"Sure." He took her hand, entwining their fingers, then led her toward the door. Ian stared at them until they'd disappeared into the main hallway outside her penthouse.

She should have shaken off his hold. But really, was there any point? All this time and space between them hadn't done anything to sever their bond. What would detaching their hands do? She wasn't sure if she was more afraid of the danger lurking outside or the man stalking her in plain sight.

Was it wrong to hope he caught her and took her down beneath him?

"God, Casey." He nuzzled his scruffy chin against her

temple, breathing deep, smelling her hair as he backed her against the wall. "It's so good to see you again."

Though it was probably a major mistake, she put her arms around him and squeezed. Regardless of how they'd left things, he'd been one of her only friends growing up. The person she had confided in. The one she ran to when things were shittier than usual. The kid she'd comforted when his parents kicked him out at fourteen because they couldn't afford to support him and they figured he could take care of himself. Jace was the reason she'd survived long enough to escape. Despite how things had ended between them, she hoped he might say the same of her.

"I'm glad you're doing well for yourself," Casey said.

"Thanks. Not as good as you, though. This place is incredible."

She simply nodded, some of that lingering emptiness in her core filling with pride and joy.

"You're even more beautiful than you were before. All woman. A damn fine woman at that." He licked his lips as if he might devour her at any moment. "It's killing me not to kiss you. You know that, right?"

He directed her hand to his crotch so there was no mistaking the effect they had on each other. He was hard and as huge as she remembered. Before she ended up stroking him, right there in the semi-public space, she retracted her fingers. He clasped them in his again.

"Is it the thought of what we had that's turning you on, or the thought of what might happen tonight?" She didn't bother with coyness. "Are you planning to spend the night in my bed?"

"I've never acted like I want to be anywhere else. You're the one who left me, remember?"

"Because you weren't honest with me. Maybe you

should be now, though." She stared directly into his chestnut eyes, although she already knew the answer to her question before she asked, "Are you hoping there's room for two or three?"

He hesitated, glancing away just long enough that she realized nothing important had changed. Not their feelings, not their attraction, and not his reluctance to share that part of himself with her.

It was pointless to repeat their past, mistakes included.

Casey flicked her hands free of his. She lifted them to his chest and shoved. Hard. Yep, he was every bit as ripped as she'd thought. Fucker. "Just do your job, Jace. Forget about the rest. I guess it's true what they say...the more things change, the more they stay the same."

"Shit!" He pounded his fist against the wall above her shoulder. He would never hit her. It wasn't even a possibility. That didn't keep her from flinching at the depth of his frustration. "Don't worry, babe. I'll keep you safe. Even if you hate that it's me guarding that smoking body of yours."

Jace leaned in toward her as if he might steal a kiss, until she angled her chin away.

He chuckled, not in the least offended. "That's okay. I'm happy to chase you as long as you like. It'll only make you taste sweeter when you surrender. You remember that, right?"

It took every ounce of her willpower not to whimper. Because she did.

"See you inside, babe." Jace gave her a lusty once-over before pivoting on his boot heel and heading toward her apartment. "Take a minute to collect yourself before Ian sees you riled up like this. He won't be able to keep his hands to himself and then I'll have to shoot him, which will result in a fuck-ton of paperwork. But only a minute or I'm coming to get you. You're safer inside. I'll be watching on the security system."

Casey waited until he closed the door before she grunted and collapsed against the wall, fanning her face. Her heart had stopped racing a bit when the door beside her cracked open. She almost shouted for Jace, until she realized it was the guy she'd learned a little too much about from the papers in the safe.

Gabriel. Her ex-priest neighbor.

"I didn't mean to eavesdrop. Goliath needs to go out." He winced. "You're not afraid of dogs, are you?"

"I guess that depends on if it's a mean dog or a nice dog." She hesitated when a chocolate-brown snout poked through the open doorway not much below the door handle. "Whoa."

"Yeah, he's incredibly friendly, but enormous and completely unaware of his size. I promise I won't let him jump on you."

"Sure, I'd love to meet him." She couldn't help but grin when the dog bounded out into the hall, tail wagging like a windshield wiper in a downpour. "Hey, big guy."

The dog sniffed her outstretched hand before letting her ruffle his ears and pet his sleek coat. She laughed when he licked her.

Gabriel hit the elevator button then relaxed, letting Goliath's leash go slack. He rested his shoulders against the opposite wall from her. With one foot propped on the damask wallpaper behind him and his arms crossed, he didn't seem at all saintly. Then again, she was nothing like the person she'd been before either. Who was she to judge?

She returned her attention to him while still petting

Goliath, who must have weighed nearly as much as she did. "Nice to meet you. I'm Casey, your new neighbor. Sorry for turning the place to shit so quickly."

He chuckled. "Is everything okay? I mean, I saw the cops earlier. And that guy...he's one of them, right?"

"That was Detective Jace West." She sighed. "I think it'll be okay. I found some papers in a safe with information about the penthouses and how to access them, who lives in them, valuable items in them, stuff like that. Thought it'd be best to call it in."

"I'll keep an eye out then." He nodded. "Thanks. How about on a personal level? He bothering you? His business with you doesn't seem all that official. I'd be happy to speak with him if you like."

The man must have God on his side to even insinuate that he'd challenge Jace. Especially when Jace was in full cop mode. He'd been intimidating before. Now he'd scare anyone straight.

"He also happens to be my long-lost ex-boyfriend." She still couldn't believe he was here.

"Ah. Yep, that explains it." Gabriel chuckled. "You know he's still into you, right?"

"I hope so, because I plan to make the best of this shitty situation." She smiled, happy to find that her neighbor was pretty awesome, not at all what she would have expected based on the black and white facts about him that she'd read earlier. Extensive tattoos peeked from beneath the collar of his T-shirt.

"Casey!" Jace shouted from inside her apartment. "Time's up. Get your pretty little ass in here. Now."

"Guess I'd better go." Casey thought it might be more fun to make Jace come get her, but that would push her drama tolerance considering she'd just met Gabriel and had to live next to him from now on.

"Guess so." Gabriel tilted his head and studied her closely as he said, "If you need a break from him or a cup of sugar or someone to take a confession...whatever, feel free to come knocking on my door. Any time of day, it doesn't matter. I don't mean that in a pervy way. Just...uh, yeah...If you need something, ask. Please."

"You're the coolest priest I've ever met, Gabriel." She held out her hand and shook his.

"*Ex*-priest. But thanks."

"Sometimes the past doesn't let go of us just because we walk away from it. Ask my *ex*-boyfriend, huh?" She smiled ruefully.

"Casey!"

She rolled her eyes at Jace's escalating bellows, though Goliath's ears stood at attention.

"You may have a point. Nice to meet you." Gabriel called his dog and they piled into the elevator car that had just arrived.

"Same." Casey marched into her apartment and slammed the door, prepared to rip Jace a new one for treating her like a disobedient pet. She might have done it, too, if Ian hadn't intercepted her and distracted her until her temper faded.

6

C asey gritted her teeth as another loud thump came from the living room. She'd had to walk away after Jace and Ian took her photographs off the wall, removed the cushions from the furniture, and flipped it all over, poking and prodding to see if they could find any hidden loot. Generally, they had fucked up every single thing she'd just finished putting in order.

They're doing their job, she reminded herself.

Very thoroughly.

So far they hadn't found anything else. They had made one hell of a mess, though. With every item they cast into disarray, her anxiety ballooned. After growing up in an untidy home with little consistency, where she was at the mercy of so many things out of her control, neatness and order helped her combat anxiety.

Another crash.

Her eye twitched.

She gripped the countertop, visually tracing the veining in the solid slab of stone. Oblivious to her near-meltdown, Jace tramped over and asked, "Do you have a flashlight, babe?"

He started opening cabinets at random, letting the doors close harder than she would have liked as he realized most of them were still empty.

"I might, somewhere in this disaster. Are you sure you don't want to tear apart the boxes I brought with me, too? Maybe you could rummage it out of there before scattering the contents across the entire penthouse for me."

He paused and looked over his shoulder. "That was sarcasm, wasn't it?"

"Yes!" She raised her hands and squeezed her head between her palms to keep it from exploding. "You're driving me nuts. I mean, I know you have to look. But can't you do it in a more organized and methodical fashion?"

"Hey, calm down. We're going to put everything back. Promise." He held his hands out in surrender.

"Not exactly like it was." She tried hard not to hyperventilate. Truth was, it was freaking her out. Having him here was bad enough. The disruption to her life, the home she'd been barely adjusting to, and now this…it was too much. "Maybe I should book a hotel room until this is over."

"You could. I would still prefer that. To be honest, though, we don't know how long the investigation will take or when—or even *if*—someone will make a move. You might have to get used to having roomies for a while."

She hadn't considered that.

She froze.

Jace didn't. He sidled closer. "There's no need to panic. I'm going to take care of you, Casey. Did you think I've forgotten how badly you need order and control in your life? Or how hard it gets you off when you surrender that power to your lover? To *me*."

A flashback to the first time he'd ever tied her up burst into her memory. They'd been fooling around in a mostly rusted abandoned bus near the lake. He'd grabbed his belt and lashed her arms together behind her back. She'd come before he'd even started fucking her, and too many times to count after. He'd had to carry her home that night since she was boneless and wasted on pleasure.

He came up behind her and wrapped his arms around her waist. His hands latched onto her wrists and held tight. "I'll take every bit of this fear inside you and turn it into something special, something amazing, if you'll let me. You're going to let me, aren't you?"

Casey shivered in his grasp.

Fuck him. "That's not playing fair."

"Nope, sure isn't. I prefer to play dirty." He kissed her neck then, making her knees weak. She sagged in his hold. He cradled her against his chest easily. "So do you, even if I'm the only one who knows it."

Casey jerked when Ian hopped over a pile of papers and landed in the kitchen, hunting for who knew what. "Oops. I didn't realize you two were...whatever you're doing. Should I go take a walk around the block or something?"

"No," they both said in unison.

She tried to break free of Jace. He didn't let her go. Not this time.

"You might as well stay and hear what I have to say," Jace explained.

"Because it impacts him too, doesn't it? What you do with me." Casey looked over her shoulder at Jace. He loosened his hold until she could turn around face him.

"You two are more than just partners on the force, aren't you?"

Ian didn't make a sound. The intensity of his stare could have cut right through the safe in the library, no locksmith needed. How much did he have riding on how today turned out?

"Yes." At least Jace didn't try to deny it this time, like he had when she'd confronted him with rumors she'd picked up while trying to keep her mom from passing out in the bar bathroom one night. She'd overheard one of the regulars bragging to her friend about how Jace had fucked her along with another, older guy she'd been dating. Casey had recognized the guy's name as someone who'd offered Jace a place to crash for a while during his couch-surfing days.

At first Casey hadn't believed it. Then, when that blabbermouth had described—in painstaking detail—the way he fucked and places he liked to be touched, Casey had thought he'd cheated on her. She'd left her mom to drink herself into oblivion so at least one of them would be happy, then stormed home to confront Jace.

When she'd unleashed on him, he hadn't denied having a threesome, except he'd sworn he'd never cheated on her. Never wanted another person after they'd hooked up. He'd said it was something he'd tried in the past. For god's sake, when he'd been just fifteen. And that he'd never do it again.

She could see the truth in his eyes, though.

He'd *wanted* to do it again. Just not with her.

In that moment, she had realized she couldn't be everything he needed the way he was for her. It devastated her. Doubly so when he refused her suggestion that they try it together.

First he'd raged that no other man would touch her, that he wouldn't loan her out to anyone like someone who didn't mean anything to him. Then he started questioning whether she wanted to hook up with other guys. When she convinced him she'd only suggested it so he could be happy, he swung in the other direction, insisting that he wouldn't let her fuck someone else just so he could get off on it. Nothing she'd said had convinced him otherwise.

From any direction she attacked the problem, it only grew. Their fighting escalated until she knew it was the kind of clash they'd never recover from.

That one secret. That single hidden desire had shattered them.

She couldn't see any way to satisfy them both.

Casey refused to make Jace miserable. Couldn't live with his eventual resentment. So she'd given him up. Walked away and left her heart behind, because that was the only honorable thing to do.

"You were right. I was wrong." He rested his forehead on hers for a moment. The weight of his regret bore down on her. "As much as I loved you, for some fucked up reason I need this in my life. Maybe it's because of how we were raised, with my dad hurting my mom and all his other girlfriends, like taking his anger out on them was going to change our situation. It freaks me out thinking I might hurt someone, even by accident. I can't let go completely unless there's someone else there. Someone I trust to take care of my woman. It's just the way I am. And it would only have hurt you worse if we'd gotten more involved, married, lived together, had kids, whatever, before I realized exactly how screwed up I am."

"You still don't get it, do you?" She tore herself from his hold. When she teetered, off balance from the overdose of hormones and grief he'd administered, Ian was there to steady her.

"I'm a freak, yeah. So?"

"It pissed me off more that you didn't trust me enough to confide your fantasies in me when I bared *everything* to you. You didn't think I could handle it." She shook her head, still wounded by his blatant assumption that she would reject him. That she wasn't as generous or accepting as he'd always been of her and her quirks. And mostly, that he thought less of her than the women he'd shared with a friend before he'd settled for her.

"What?" Jace blinked a few times, as if struggling to think clearly when so much of his blood flow had been diverted below his belt.

"She's saying you fucked up by hiding what you like and that you stomped all over her pride by making it seem like other playmates could give you something she couldn't, you idiot." Ian wrapped an arm around her. He had tucked her to his side when he noticed her fists balling up and tears prickling her eyes.

Oh no, she would not shed even one more over this jerk. No way.

"You can't seriously want me to think you would have been into it? A three-way?" Jace practically snorted. "No way. I saw your face when you told me what you'd heard that night. That wasn't lust. It was fear and disgust."

"I was naïve, Jace. I didn't know relationships like that existed. Not as something more than a sordid brag from a man who considered fucking two women at once some kind of boost to his manhood. When I found out what you'd done, it was a shock. And yes, I was livid when I thought you'd cheated on me. I expected that of men in general, but not of you. Where we came from, hardly anyone was faithful except for Mr. and Mrs. Wilton, who'd been together since the Great Depression or some shit. That's where my reactions came from. It didn't have to be that way. You made it so much worse by hiding what you wanted until I'd already formed an idea of what our future looked like. Together. You and me against the world."

He nodded then, a lot more slowly. Maybe it was sinking in, now that they were distanced from the emotions that had swept over them both like a tidal wave, destroying everything they'd built together. "So when you heard I liked to share..."

"It felt like you didn't want me as bad as I wanted you. That I wasn't enough for you, so you'd found someone else. Something more intense than I could give. I'd only ever been with you. Only knew what you'd taught me. Maybe I was a slow learner. Maybe you wanted another woman to do it right." She snarled then. "I'd rip a bitch's head off with my bare hands if you wanted to fuck her in front of me. So I couldn't understand at first why that might be different for you. I reacted badly. And...well..."

"I did too, Casey. I'm sorry. For all of it." His shoulders drooped. "All I ever wanted was to make you as happy as possible, including in bed. That night, when you confronted me, I knew I couldn't give you everything. Not by myself. The thought of unleashing all the nasty parts of me without someone else to rein me in and keep you safe if I went too far—"

He couldn't finish.

"Hey, man. It's okay." Ian put a hand on Jace's shoulder then, shaking him a little. "You never would have put her at risk."

Jace nodded again, then looked straight into her eyes.

"So when you left me, I thought it was what was best for you, even if it nearly killed me."

Could it possibly have been as painful for him as it had been for her? She'd ripped her own soul out and left it behind in the dust.

For the first time, she saw how badly she'd injured him—his ego and the tender emotions she hadn't realized were only blossoming inside him then. He may have fucked plenty of other people before her. In ménages, even. But he'd never loved them. She could see that plainly now that she was older and wiser.

"I'm sorry too, Jace." She lunged across the gap between them, grateful when he opened his arms to her.

"We weren't ready," he mumbled against her hair. His arms crushed her even as they shook.

"I think we might be now."

7

J ace balked. "I don't know, Casey."

His hesitance struck her as rejection. Again.

Fortunately Ian was there to singlehandedly stop the runaway train of their dysfunction before it could derail their reconnection. When her spine stiffened, he was there, caressing her shoulder. "He's afraid of losing you twice."

"Well, I'll put it this way." She propped her hands on her hips. "If you want to fuck me again, you're going to have to do it with Ian. I'm not going to use you, or take what I need without giving you the same. No way. Either I'll like it, too, or I won't. I'm not promising anything. But there's only one way to find out."

Jace practically growled. "Babe, be careful. Hearing you say shit like that does things to me. Things I can't control."

"That's exactly why you have me." Ian grinned as he looked between them. "Don't worry, Jace. I've got your back. You're not going to shut this down for us both, are you? I can already tell this is going to be next level."

The guys exchanged a look that Casey tried desperately to interpret. She felt something pass between them. Some sort of pact, or maybe an ultimatum. Maybe they needed her too, to keep their arrangement alive.

"So you do this all the time now?" she wondered aloud before realizing how her question might come off. "I'm not judging. I just think I deserve to fully understand the situation this time. So I'm not surprised, or disappointed, when it's all on the table. Is this like a thing you do every once in a while, or is every time you sleep with someone a twofer? That's fair to ask, right?"

"You can ask us anything. Any time," Ian assured her. "I'll make sure he's completely transparent if that's what you need."

She nodded, her apprehension fading. He got her, understood her uneasiness and didn't hold it against her. Where Jace might bulldoze the truth and leverage her desire to evade tough topics, Ian confronted them head on without blowing up. He was easy to negotiate with.

An important skill in any relationship, it could be critical in a complex arrangement like the one they were about to explore together.

"Answer her, Jace," Ian encouraged.

"Yeah. This is how it always is now. I don't fuck women solo. It stresses me out and takes away from my enjoyment, worrying about monitoring myself while I'm trying to let go of all the bullshit in my head. I thought I could change for you." Jace winced. "I love you. *Loved* you, I mean."

Ian cleared his throat with a cough that sounded decidedly like, "Bullshit."

Jace rounded on his partner. "Seriously. You're not helping."

44

"Funny, I think I am. For whatever reason, we're all here in the same place, at the same time, with chemistry as powerful as those lights on the Brooklyn Bridge over there." Ian shook his head. "This could be the only chance you have to fix your past mistakes. As your friend, I won't stand by and watch you blow it. Be honest with her. Completely. Maybe if you had been before, you wouldn't have lost her in the first place."

For a moment, Casey thought Jace might lunge at Ian. Take a swing at him. She could imagine them tumbling around, smashing things in her elegant home as if it were one of the seedy, smoke-filled bars she'd grown up in. Ones where Jace had proved over and over that he was strong enough, and cared enough, to keep her safe even when her own mother wasn't.

He'd broken a few stray hands that had grabbed her tits and ass before she even knew what those parts of her anatomy were good for. Then once she'd started playing pool, hustling the drunk bastards who'd underestimated her time and time again, he'd taken care of anyone who'd gotten angry that she'd used their paycheck to buy Jace and her some real food or to pad her pie-in-the-sky college fund.

She'd never admit it out loud, but watching him stick up for her, protect her, and go to battle for her had turned her on. It spoke to something primal inside her that craved security. The kind she'd tried to build for herself with her single-minded pursuit of her career.

Casey was never going back to that life. Couldn't survive it.

Instead of breaking Ian's perfect, sculpted nose, Jace took a deep breath, then faced her. It shocked her. He listened to Ian, actually took his advice instead of succumbing to his white-hot temper. She'd never seen him come back from somewhere near his flashpoint before.

Jace unlocked his jaw and said in a gravelly rasp, "I have thought about you every day since you left. You never left my mind. Or my heart. There, happy?"

He glared at Ian.

Okay, so he was still Jace at the core. He'd just learned how to adapt. She could handle that. Because there were things she had to say. Things that would have set the old Jace off into an argument where neither of them heard the other no matter how loud they screamed.

"I believed you before, when you told me that. But it's hard to now. You didn't fight very hard for me. You let me leave. You never once called, or emailed, or anything. That hurt the most. Knowing you didn't even try…"

"Hey." Ian rubbed her shoulder, tucking her closer to his strength and heat. She accepted his solace when she couldn't have gone to Jace that easily. Not with the weight of everything between them. "I hate to break it to you, but I don't think you've got this one straight. Jace has never really let you go. Not all the way. He compares every woman we're with to you, and they come up lacking. It's been causing some issues lately that we can talk about some other time, okay?"

"Shit!" Jace glared at his partner and best friend.

"In fact, I'd venture to say that the harder he fell for you, the *more* he wanted to explore ménage because he knew how much pleasure it would bring you." Ian smiled softly. "It takes a lot for a guy to swallow his pride and ask another man to help him drive his lover crazy, don't you think?"

Well, she'd never quite thought of it that way.

What once had seemed illicit and warped now seemed generous and romantic, in a way.

"But once he realized he was never going to end up in a traditional relationship but believed that's all you wanted, he didn't feel it was right to try to lure you back to a life you weren't interested in." Ian laid it all out when Jace never could have explained so clearly without getting upset. "Now that he knows you're open to the idea, there's going to be no stopping him from having you. From *us* having you."

Both she and Jace were silent, evaluating each other and the man standing between them, the one helping them find their way back to each other.

"If I'm wrong, you can stop me from kissing her. Just say the word, partner." Ian cupped her chin and angled her face toward his. His eyes were a deep brown that mesmerized her. He was gentle and coaxing where Jace would have been forceful. He was sweet, and impossible to resist. "You can stop me too, Casey. If you want."

That bastard chuckled.

But he wasn't wrong.

She didn't want him to stop. Not now when she could sense the heat of his well-muscled body seeping into her. Already turned on enough that she could probably come in his arms if he'd hold her close enough and let her grind against his thigh while they made out, she didn't resist.

"Fuck, that's hot." Jace groaned as he watched them introduce themselves to each other in this way. Since they'd only have one first kiss, she tried her best to make it count.

Casey parted her lips and relaxed into Ian's grip. He took advantage, teasing the tip of her tongue with his as he glided his mouth across hers. They kissed until she grew dizzy from lack of oxygen.

At some point, Jace had come closer so he could stroke his fingers through her hair while she kissed the shit out of his partner. If only she'd known how perfect this could feel, she would have found him and apologized a long time ago. If only he'd shown her...

"What?" Ian asked, nearly as breathless as she felt. "What's that frown for?"

"I was a foolish girl back then. I didn't understand. I wasted so much time." She sighed, looking over her shoulder at Jace. "Now I'm a woman, fully capable of making my own decisions about what will or will not happen in my bedroom."

"I can see that." Ian inched forward, trapping her between him and Jace. She didn't stop him.

"It's been a while since I found someone I was excited to be with. Since the thought of dating and sex sounded more like fun and less like an interview or a chore." She leaned toward Ian, who reached out to Jace, pulling him closer. He came. If he hadn't wanted to, he could easily have resisted the light tug. "So if I want to see what this is like, I hope you'll indulge me. Even if it's just for tonight."

"I'm in," Ian said immediately.

Jace studied the two of them for a while before admitting, "I could never say no to you."

He leaned in and angled her face toward him. He held her steady as he closed the gap between them and fused his mouth to hers. She wondered if he could taste Ian's cinnamon flavor on her lips. It had been forever since she'd kissed him, and still she remembered every detail, every nuance of how he made love to her with his mouth. God, she'd missed this.

Casey couldn't say if she moaned because it felt so right or because witnessing their interaction was making Ian harder. His growing erection nudged her hip.

She'd never been one for mind games before.

With Jace West, she had no sense of self-preservation or restraint.

When it came to the ex-love-of-her-life who—she was coming to realize—might be the current-love-of-her-life, she could only fight with fiery passion.

"So what do you say, Jace?" Ian cocked his head and flashed a disarming grin before making absolutely sure they were all in agreement. "*Su señorita es mi señorita, no?*"

Jace broke their contact and swallowed hard. He paused, only the rapid rise and fall of his chest betraying how high the stakes were for him. Finally, he nodded.

Ian lifted Casey. He spun her around a few times before moving toward the tall counter of the kitchen island. While he had her in the air, Jace reached over and raised her skirt, bunching it around her waist in one fluid motion just before Ian set her down. The cool stone beneath her ass shocked her. She gasped.

Ian grinned and tucked the loose tendrils of hair behind her ear. "I can't wait to hear you make those noises while I'm eating you. Jace told me how loud and sweet you are when you come. Let's see if he was telling the truth, huh?"

What? Was that where this was heading? Of course it was. These two guys weren't the sort to take things slow or be satisfied with a few lusty kisses. No, they were going to dive right in. They were doing this. Today. Right now.

Casey bit her lip and nodded eagerly.

Jace set one hand on each of her knees and yanked,

spreading her wide open. "Don't make me a liar, babe. Show Ian how fucking delicious you are."

She braced her hands behind her, flat on the counter, then leaned back on straight-locked arms. Her gaze flew to Jace's, suddenly worried. What if she let him down? What if she could only lose herself to rapture with him? Could she fuck up his bond with Ian?

Suddenly it felt like there was a lot she hadn't considered before selfishly jumping at this chance.

Jace called his friend's attention to her reaction. "Ian, help."

Casey looked away and down, embarrassed by their scrutiny.

"Sorry, that was a lot of pressure to put on you," Ian said as he stroked her legs from the tops of her thighs to her knees, then down her calves. Over and over. "We only said those things because there's no doubt in our minds that you're going to blow us away. You already have by being so brave and open to this."

She drew a deep breath as the tension melted from her bones. "Okay."

"Here, let me prove it to you." Ian walked his fingers higher this time, to the waistband of her lacy panties. She lifted her ass so he could slide them down then over her knees. From there, they floated to the floor.

"I can smell you already, babe. You're as fucking hot as I remembered," Jace rasped in her ear as he covered her face with kisses. When he claimed her mouth, it was nothing like the liquid exchange she'd had with Ian.

Jace sealed his mouth over hers and plundered, distracted her with deep contact, the pulls of his mouth as he sucked on her tongue, and the sharp nips of his teeth sprinkled in, keeping her on edge. While she focused on him, Ian bent lower and began to kiss and lick a trail up her leg.

It felt surreal and so fucking great to have an extra set of hands and a second mouth on her skin, driving her beyond reason or doubt. She let go, quit thinking, and committed herself to simply reacting. When they did something that sent sparks up her spine, she allowed her moans to break free from her throat without suppressing them or worrying about propriety as she had with other lovers she'd had while pursuing a partner appropriate for the sophisticated woman she aimed to be.

What an idiot! Appropriate was definitely not the criteria a woman should use to pick a lover.

While Ian progressed up her thighs, tormenting her with his slow pace, Jace took things up another notch. He shoved his hand down the front of her tank top, pushed the cups of her bra beneath her breasts, then filled his palm with one. He kneaded it as he devoured her cries.

When he pinched her nipple, hard, her hips rocked off the counter.

Ian took that as a sign. "Almost there. Is this where you want my mouth next?"

He swiped a finger along her slit, brushing his thumb lightly over her clit.

Casey wrenched her mouth from Jace long enough to shout, "Yes!"

Jace chuckled against her swollen lips before resuming his torture. Ian, however, delivered on the arousal he'd amplified with his skilled seduction. He slid his hands beneath her thighs then yanked, drawing her to the edge of the counter.

Fear of falling might have distracted her from her pleasure under ordinary circumstances. Not right then.

Because Jace would never let her fall. She reclined against the arm he'd slung around her back, holding her in place for his partner.

Fuck yes.

Ian licked her pussy softly at first, then with stronger intention. He dipped between her folds, escalating the flick of his tongue over her clit at the top of each pass. When he surrounded her clit with his lips and sucked lightly, in rhythmic pulses, she knew she wasn't going to make either man wait long to hear her crying out their names as she shuddered in climax.

Jace took one look at her and chuckled. "I told you. He's a pro."

Speaking was beyond her. She fisted Jace's shirt in her hands and drew him toward her. Could he see how deeply this touched her, finally correcting the biggest regret of her life? That alone had her soaring.

He switched his hand to her other breast, and when even that wasn't enough, he dropped his head to one while he massaged the other.

Casey looked down at the two men working her over. They complemented each other beautifully, making her muscles quiver with the effort of withholding her orgasm.

"Don't you dare," Jace rumbled against her breast before biting her harder than before. "Give him what he wants, what he's working so hard for. There's more where that came from, don't worry. Come for us, Casey."

As he ordered her, and her body responded, Ian did his best to make sure she could obey.

He inserted one thick finger into her pussy and curled it so that he pressed just right, trapping her G-spot against her pubic bone. She couldn't stop it.

Casey screamed. She came with a gush that might

have embarrassed her if Ian hadn't shoved his face tighter against her as if to capture every last drop of her pleasure.

"Fuck, that's so hot." Jace put one hand on the counter and vaulted on top of it.

She'd remember to object to his boots on the food prep area later. He cradled her head in his palm while she rode out the rest of her climax. When the other hand fumbled at the fly of his jeans, she realized he planned to feed her his cock.

Casey opened her mouth and leaned forward, eager to taste him again. Especially if she could bring him even half as much bliss as Jace had brought her by sharing her with Ian.

Somewhere in the recesses of her mind, she heard something that didn't involve Jace or Ian. She simply didn't care. Except it didn't stop.

Ian lifted his head from where he was sipping at her, bringing her down from the spasms still wringing her dry. "Someone's at the door."

"Casey?"

8

Casey clapped her hand over her mouth, trying to contain the last of her echoing cries. It was no use. She'd practically flown apart right there on her kitchen counter. The proof of her pleasure reverberated off the hard surfaces of the gleaming kitchen.

"Casey? Are you okay?" Everly shouted through the door.

Casey buried her face in her hands. There was no use in pretending she wasn't actually home. Hell, as the building manager, Everly was likely to call the police or use her master key to gain entry. That would be awkward for everyone. Having Jace and Ian's co-workers taking notes about the "disturbance" in her apartment was unacceptable.

"I've got this." Ian kissed her thigh, then wiped his mouth with his forearm before looking at Jace. "But you'd better get down and zip up."

Jace grimaced and attempted to tuck his incredibly stiff cock back into his jeans. She reached up to help draw the denim together. Her knuckles brushed the warm flesh of his hard-on, which jerked.

"You're not helping, babe," he groaned.

"Casey!" Everly yelled louder.

"Coming," Casey responded shakily.

Ian laughed out loud when Jace stepped back, finished the job, then leapt down from the countertop before lifting Casey off it, too. Her skirt fell into place as Jace adjusted her shirt and bra. Casey finger combed her hair and tried to stop shaking with pleasure.

Meanwhile, Ian jogged to the door and opened it. "Hey, Gabriel. Everly. What can we do for you?"

Nobody—not even the non-cop civilians—was going to buy Ian's innocent greeting.

"We were going to ask if you were interested in checking out the movie playing on the big screen in the park tonight. But...I can see you've got other plans." Gabriel winced.

"Sorry, I thought I heard Casey scream." Everly blushed. "I made him come with me to see if you were all right."

"You did hear her scream." Jace's puffed-up chest made it clear he wasn't ashamed they'd nearly drowned her in ecstasy. "And she's fine. Great, I think."

Casey smacked his gut and hissed, "Stop it."

The instant she showed her ire, Goliath growled from where he stood between Gabriel and Everly. As big as he was, it was an intimidating warning.

"It's okay, boy." Gabriel patted his head and tugged on his leash.

"You made him mad at me." Jace practically pouted. He'd always wanted a dog of his own. When she'd left, he'd inherited her goldfish. It wasn't the same, though.

Casey took Jace's hand and led him toward Goliath while speaking sweetly to the dog. "Thanks, Goliath, but he's a friend. See?"

She held Jace's hand out to the dog, who sniffed it then smashed his face against it, begging for attention. Ian joined in as they lavished Goliath with affection. The dog seemed like he was in heaven at the center of all their attention.

She completely understood the feeling...and couldn't wait to experience even more of it.

"So, uh, what have you been up to?" Everly asked, sort of awkwardly.

The guys looked to Casey, and she shrugged. No sense in hiding what everyone already knew. "Christening the kitchen counter..."

Gabriel snorted.

Immediately, she blushed. "That's probably a horrible thing to say to an actual holy man, right?"

He laughed. "Not really. It's not like you murdered someone. Besides, these days I'm a sinner like everyone else."

Everly flashed her a discreet thumbs-up. "In that case, I guess we should leave you alone."

It was clear from her curious stares at the three of them that she was trying to figure out who was doing who.

Casey saved them the effort of wondering what was happening behind closed doors. She asked quietly, "Hey, Gabriel?"

"Yes?" He turned slowly, cocking his head.

"Do you think I'll go to hell if I fuck two incredibly hot cops at once?" She gnawed on her lip as if it wasn't already a near certainty that they were going to be sharing her lush California king bed tonight. It felt important that she show Jace she wasn't ashamed of him or what he was into anymore, even if it might take a little getting used to.

"Babe." Jace sounded amused, if exasperated.

"Casey," Ian hissed, his standards of decorum completely scandalized by the crass girl who still lived buried deep inside her and escaped on occasion.

To her surprise, Gabriel burst out laughing. Casey knew she'd made the right call. "Nah. And if you do, at least I'll have company down below."

"In that case, it'll be worth it." Casey couldn't believe she was considering it—shit, had already decided. It was completely unlike her to reach an impulsive verdict, especially about something so outrageous. Her neglected sex drive had roared back to life, smothering her mind's objections. Especially after discovering how talented Ian's mouth was. If he could do that to her with his lips and tongue, what could he do with his cock?

She sure wanted to find out. Pronto.

"If you need anything—you know other than, like, condoms or a spare handcuff key or something—we'll be across the hall in my *very* sound-proofed penthouse with the stereo turned up. So make sure you call ahead." Garbriel grinned when Everly chuckled.

"Thanks." Casey melted a little, even though she tried to stay tough. Maybe she could fit in here better than she thought. Maybe she could belong. Maybe her life was about to take a turn that would enrich her existence far more than the material possessions she'd bought herself through hard work and a fear of failure had. "Seriously, I appreciate everything you two have done to make me feel welcome here."

"I do, too. Now it's time for Casey to come inside." Jace

turned, then said over his shoulder, "Thanks for checking on her, guys. See you later."

"Sorry, he's concerned about her being any more exposed than necessary right now." Ian smoothed over Jace's brusqueness, as usual.

"I can understand that." Everly winked. She and Gabriel were gracious as they headed toward his apartment with Goliath on their heels. "Enjoy yourselves."

"We will, guaranteed," Jace promised low enough that Casey hoped only she'd heard.

"Thanks. Bye." She waved then held her hand out to Ian. He took it, bringing it to his lips for a casual kiss that spiked her temperature. Then he used the connection to escort her inside, and locked the door behind them.

Meanwhile, Jace grumbled, "No, that's not what I meant. I want Casey to myself. Well, to *ourselves* for the rest of the night. No more interruptions. I've waited ten fucking years for this. That's long enough."

9

Though they could have resumed where they'd left off the moment Everly, Gabriel, and Goliath left, the guys had reverted to cop mode instead. Casey couldn't say if it was that the mood had been shattered or if their unintended timeout had shaken them awake from the fantasy they'd been reenacting.

Or maybe the guys were pretending to be well behaved because they thought that's what she would prefer. Either way, she was getting antsier—and hornier— by the minute.

Sure, the orgasm Ian had given her had been incredible. No one had ever gone down on her like that before. Not even Jace. But she needed more. The sweaty, rhythmic slapping of bodies straining toward completion together. Watching the guys shatter as completely as she had.

She'd missed that. Unbridled passion and sex so good she didn't give a fuck what she looked or sounded like while she was getting it on. Not since Jace had she been that uninhibited. Free.

Suddenly, she thought she might die if she didn't experience that complete liberation again soon. Jace's logic had sunk in, too, though. It would be nice to have someone else there. Someone like Ian, who was every bit as passionate, yet far more controlled. Someone who'd make sure they didn't harm each other again. Guardrails to keep them from rocketing over the edge of a cliff.

Casey barely resisted tapping her toe as the guys finished their search through her apartment, this time being more aware of their impact on her environment. When they'd reached the final area and cleared it, she thought for sure they would make their move.

Instead, Ian asked her, "Do you have food in the house? I can cook us something for dinner."

They'd ordered lunch, as she usually did. But she had some basics on hand.

She wasn't about to turn down his offer. "Hopefully it's enough for you to throw something together."

Jace rubbed his stomach. "Ian can make something out of nothing. I remember the days when we'd run out of money a few days before payday. He'd take a packet of ramen noodles or a can of SpaghettiOs and doctor it up until it seemed like a feast. I don't know how he did it, but we never went hungry like I had back home."

Ian shrugged. "It's not that hard. Let me see what you've got."

Casey spent the next half hour admiring him as he turned an opened box of pasta, some leftover grilled chicken, a couple vegetables, and a dash of spices into a delicious herbed pasta in a light butter sauce that made her sorry, for once, that she didn't have any wine in the house.

"This is delicious, thank you," she told him with her

mouth half full. Manners be damned.

"You're welcome." He cleaned his own plate. "Need to feed you so you have enough energy for tonight."

And there it was.

Her body lit up like a neon sign flickering to life. "Tonight, as in right now. Right?" She stood up from the table fast enough that her chair squeaked against the floor.

Jace laughed and hugged his stomach. "I'm glad I'm not the only one dying over here."

Even Ian seemed relieved. "I was trying not to pressure you. This is new and unexpected."

Casey couldn't deny that. It was exciting, too. "It's kind of like having sex with a stranger. Thrilling, but not as petrifying because I know Jace and trust him, despite everything. He wouldn't let just anyone touch me. I'm sure of that."

"Same for me." Ian's smile turned wolfish then. "It's an honor for such a gorgeous, powerful quasi-stranger to invite me into her bed. I plan to make sure you're not sorry you did."

She turned to Jace. "Where did you find him? Can we keep him? Please?"

Both of the guys laughed at that.

"We ended up as roommates while going through the police academy. I couldn't afford to live in the city on my own and Ian had inherited a sweet townhouse in Brooklyn from his grandmother. I moved in and helped him renovate on the weekends. Afterward, we'd go out together. It didn't take long to realize we had similar tastes in women and what we liked to do with them. To them. For them. So we just kept doing what was working for us." Jace shrugged.

Ian hesitated as if he might add something else. Instead he let it go and angled himself toward her. "We make a good team. On the force and elsewhere."

"I did notice you tend to have a good cop, bad cop thing going." She grinned as she leaned in closer to Ian. It was odd to be so attracted to another man in Jace's presence. The impact of his stare only turned her on more. She ran her hand down Ian's neck. "Maybe you could demonstrate some more of your partnering skills."

Jace cursed under his breath. In her peripheral vision, she saw him cup his crotch as if his dick was about to bust through his pants. Perfect. Riling him up was exactly what she wanted.

"I should clean up the kitchen first," Ian murmured, though he didn't seem very interested in the prospect.

"Fuck the dishes. Better yet, fuck me." Casey turned to Jace. "Stop torturing me, please."

She craved the passion he would rain on her. The rough, raw claiming he'd treated her to in the past. At the same time, she was also drawn to the suave style of Ian's more sophisticated approach. Asking her to pick a favorite would be like forcing her to choose between salty caramel and birthday cake ice cream. Casey loved them both. Craved them and devoured them at every opportunity, even if it meant an extra half hour at the gym burning it off.

Somehow she knew that once she slept with these men, they would become her new guilty pleasure. At least fucking was solid exercise. So that meant more ice cream, too. Yassss!

Ian was everything she'd looked for in guys since Jace. Ones she'd been unsatisfied with or bored by. Jace brought the edge that could slice her open again if she wasn't careful. Together...

They could be the perfect pairing.

She stood on her tiptoes and wrapped her hands around Ian's neck. He put one arm low across her back. His fingers rested on the top swell of her ass, drawing her toward him, supporting her as she took what she wanted from him.

Casey kissed him sweetly, slowly, yet no less passionately than she had made out with Jace earlier. He hummed as his tongue stole between her lips.

"Carry her to her room," Jace ordered, then led the way.

Casey squealed when Ian scooped her into his arms and followed.

She was thankful they were going to do this someplace softer this time, because she planned to be at it for a while and the counter wasn't exactly the most comfortable spot in the house. When they entered her room, Ian set her down carefully.

"Strip her," Jace demanded. "I want to see her naked this time. Have nothing in our way when we want to touch her, lick her, fuck her."

Casey was about to reach for her own clothes then. She couldn't get them off fast enough.

She didn't get the chance. Ian was there, walking her tank up her torso slowly, teasing Jace with the deliberate strip tease neither she nor Jace would have had the patience for. It built the anticipation to unbearable levels.

When finally he'd pulled the shirt fully over her head and arms, he started again at her waist, this time tugging her skirt off bit by bit. She hadn't bothered putting her panties back on after their earlier liaison.

Jace cursed. "I've been hard all afternoon knowing you were bare under that."

"Underwear is overrated." She grinned. "I like to go commando a lot."

"Now I'll always wonder," Ian sighed.

"Feel free to check whenever you like." She laughed. How was this so easy? So fun and stress-free?

"Maybe I will, with my tongue." Ian seemed like he might opt for a second round of oral sex. He must really enjoy eating pussy, or at least hers. Either that or he didn't realize that the entire afternoon—hell, the entire day—with them had been one giant bout of mental foreplay.

"Thank you, but...will you hate me if I say I need the real thing this time?" She shook her hair out behind her then ran her hands from her chest to her pussy, which ached with the desire to be stretched and stuffed full of cock. "Soon."

"Of course not." He kissed her softly, making sure she could feel the proof of his arousal against her belly. "I was only trying to be polite. I'm ready whenever you are."

Ian exchanged a glance with Jace. Moments later, they were both stripping off their clothes without ceremony. Rushed or not, they had damn near perfect physiques. Ian was taller and sleeker than Jace, his chest and abdomen worthy of one of the enormous perfume ads that stretched into the sky in Times Square.

She'd fork over serious amounts of hard-earned cash for any product with him on it. Damn.

On the other hand, Jace had a stature that would have been equally appropriate on a tiger or a pit bull. His muscles were thick and bunched as he moved. She stared at the difference a decade had wrought on his physique, admiring every single bulge that hadn't been there before.

Could she truly be lucky enough to have them both?

Wait. A thought occurred to her. "Do you do this one at a time or are you expecting me to be some ultra-coordinated porn queen?"

"Whatever comes naturally." Ian wrapped his arms around her and kissed her temple. "Don't think so much. Let us make you feel good."

"You already are." She leaned into his hold, closing her eyes.

Jace must have come closer while she absorbed Ian's comforting embrace. Without warning, his mouth pressed to hers. Skin-on-skin contact with him made her shiver. He chuckled and took advantage, toying with her rock-hard nipples for a moment.

Instinctively, she arched her spine. Her head lolled onto Ian's shoulder. Contact with both men at once threatened to overheat her. It was a completely novel experience, yet one she knew she'd never surpass in her lifetime.

This was it, as good as it got.

"Lay her on the bed on her back," Jace directed Ian. "Then do your thing."

"You ready? For sure?" Ian asked her.

"Absolutely."

Casey couldn't believe she was about to do something so reckless. And even weirder, it felt completely safe. Totally normal. Perfect, in every way.

This time she was prepared when Ian lifted her. She liked how easily he could manhandle her if he chose, and she let him. He climbed onto the bed with her, laid her down gently, then blanketed her with his amazing body.

Better already.

Casey hummed. Her toes curled against the ultra-luxurious sheets as Ian's hips settled in between her thighs. So close to where she needed him.

He stole a kiss that quickly turned into something more intense. Grinding on her while he made love to her mouth, his entire body stroked her.

Frantic, she raked her nails down his back before she realized what she'd done. He gasped and redoubled his efforts. She realized she hadn't seen even a fraction of what he was capable of yet. Ian lifted his head then and looked to Jace for direction.

"Put this on." Jace tossed a condom to Ian. She couldn't take her stare from him as he rolled the thin latex over his impressive length. She'd never been with a man as long as him. Thank god her sex toy collection had prepared her for this possibility. Or at least she hoped it had.

"Now get inside her." He smacked Ian's ass as if they were football players on a world championship team. Casey would be glad to buy them gaudy, glittering rings if their fucking lived up to the hype.

If Ian didn't bury himself inside her soon, she was going to roll him to his back, hop on top, and ride him like the wild, wannabe cowgirl she'd always been inside.

Fortunately, he didn't keep her waiting.

Ian aligned his cock with her pussy then traced the furrow between her lips, rubbing her with the blunt cap of his dick. It felt amazing and also spread her arousal, getting them both good and wet.

"Take it easy on me, will you? You're even bigger than my vibrator." She licked her lips.

"I'll see what I can do," he said with a smile.

Casey nodded. "Please."

Jace stared at his best friend as Ian began to press

deeper into her. He penetrated her the barest bit, then paused so they both could adjust to the pressure and incredible sensations.

"That's right, get in there. Open her up for me." Jace crawled onto the bed for a closer look. He knelt beside her head as he coached Ian. How could she have forgotten he was the master of dirty talk?

She peered up at him as he towered over her. One of his hands curled around his dick and began to stroke. If she strained, she might be able to...

Casey sucked on Jace's balls as Ian advanced through the tight channel of clenching muscles.

"Hell yes," Jace groaned, and fisted her hair in his hand. It only made Ian's introduction to her body that much more impactful and distracted from the slight pinch of being filled completely after a relatively long hiatus.

It didn't take long before Ian was locked as deep as possible within her. He paused to take in the show she and Jace were giving him. He obviously liked it. His cock stiffened more and flared within her. Damn.

Jace directed Casey upward. She opened her mouth wider so he could tuck the tip of his dick between her lips. Ian withdrew until he nearly slipped from her body.

She groaned.

"Don't worry, I'm not going anywhere," he promised, his voice husky.

Jace looked at him then. Without a word, they advanced in unison. They fucked her from both ends simultaneously. Casey gurgled happily around Jace's cock while her pussy spasmed, hugging Ian.

They started slowly, letting her revel in the newness of these extraordinary pleasures. But all too soon, things got serious. It seemed the guys were as desperate as her for this initial release.

Ian pumped into her, making her breasts sway. Jace covered one with his hand as he encouraged her to take him deeper into her throat. She loved the feel of his heat and weight on her tongue as she laved him, savoring the flavor that seemed at once familiar and delicious to her.

What was better than treating your man to a blowjob but getting fucked at the same time? Win-win. No sacrifices for anyone. She couldn't wait to make him come and know that she'd finally been able to give him what he'd always needed.

The thought made her eyes water with pure joy.

Her pussy clamped down on Ian. It would only take one or two more of those perfectly placed thrusts to tip her over the edge into a mind-blowing orgasm.

Jace cheered Ian on. "Fuck her good. Deep. Make her come then shoot your load. I'll take it from here. It's okay to let go. I promise, I'll give her more."

Damn, he knew how to influence Ian. Hearing that she'd be cared for, he surrendered. He began to fuck her with the frantic lunges of a madman. His pelvis pressed against her clit with every thrust.

Casey couldn't think of anything except the feel of him plowing deeper and faster into her. She increased her suction on Jace's dick, trying to make him join Ian in release. She'd drink him down, swallow, and smile up at him, begging for more.

He'd always loved that.

Ian traced her lips where they hugged Jace's cock.

Then he shouted her name. The pure pleasure in his cry ratcheted her need higher. Casey trembled along the entire length of her body, then she shattered. She convulsed around Ian even as Jace withdrew his cock, probably for his own safety.

She couldn't control the full-body tremors that wracked her.

Especially when Ian joined her, pumping his release into the condom he wore. She wished he had flooded her pussy instead. Would Jace fuck her right after Ian had flooded her pussy?

Someday, she hoped to find out.

Casey kept climaxing, wringing every bit of come from Ian's balls before she went limp. Ian collapsed over her, kissing her sweetly while his ass bunched in a series of small jerks that kept the embers of her passion glowing inside her.

"My turn." Jace nudged Ian's shoulder. He sighed, then withdrew, making Casey moan and whimper.

"It's okay, babe." Jace grinned at her mindless pleasure and the animalistic response she had to him and his partner team-fucking her. "I've got more for you, if you can take it."

She was never one to shy away from a challenge.

Casey reached out to him as Ian rolled off her and lay against her side. He hugged her to him, whispering his thanks and endless praise as he caressed her entire body, making her eager for Jace's cock.

She never would have imagined she could recover that quickly or that she'd be just as needy for Jace after a monumental release, but she was.

Sometime while she was preoccupied, Jace had put on protection. Good thing someone was thinking about practical stuff. All she could think about was cramming him inside her and stealing another orgasm like the one Ian had given her.

Where Ian had the lead in length, Jace was way ahead in girth. Each of their cocks made for a distinct sensation. She cried out when Jace fitted himself to her and began to slide inside. It had been wise of them to let Ian fuck her first. It made Jace's long-awaited reentry into her body smooth and incredibly pleasurable.

She flashed back to the night he'd taken her virginity. Though it had hurt, he'd quickly morphed her discomfort into bliss. Tonight, there was only pleasure. Could the rest of their relationship be like that too? Only smooth sailing from here on out?

Would they even have a relationship after tonight?

She couldn't worry about that now.

Not when he began to shuttle between her legs, cursing and grunting as he made himself at home in her body. Again.

Jace didn't ask, didn't warn, didn't baby her. He fucked.

After she'd adjusted to having him inside her again, he pulled out, leaving her empty and begging for more.

"Just a second, babe," he promised. Then he gripped her waist and rotated her so that she had to throw out her hands and balance on all fours to keep from smashing face-first into the mattress. Ian steadied her and kept her from falling. He slid beneath her so she was nestled against his chest.

Ian whispered encouragement to her and stroked her hair back while Jace really got into things. He fucked her from behind, his hips banging into her ass, shoving her deeper into Ian's embrace.

Her other lover held her steady, kissed her deeply, then reached under her to rub her clit.

Oh, fuck.

Casey couldn't speak, could hardly think. All she

could do was let them take control of her pleasure and try to withstand the lashes of rapture that spurred her toward another climax. She never wanted this to end.

"Shit. I'm not going to last, Casey." Jace bit her shoulder. "Not tonight. Not this first time. Not when you're everything I've ever dreamed you would be. Thank you. Fuck. I need you. I always have."

His desperate confession undid her.

Casey hadn't thought it possible to come so hard three times in one day. She was thrilled to be proven wrong. Each of her orgasms seemed better than the last.

Dangerous.

Because she was already becoming addicted to the happiness they could bring her. Worse, she didn't care. She refused to let doubt or fear take away from the glory of the moment.

She screamed as Jace surrounded her waist with his hands, impaled her fully, then bellowed her name as he joined her in ecstasy. He shuddered as he shot jet after jet of hot come into his condom, punctuating his orgasm with a slap on her ass that inspired another mini-orgasm of her own.

When they'd finished squeezing every bit of pleasure from each other, she drooped, right into Ian's waiting embrace. He held her tight as Jace withdrew. When Jace joined them on the pillows, Ian rotated, trapping her between the two men. She loved being bracketed by their strength and sexiness.

Physically satisfied, emotionally exhausted, and utterly overwhelmed by the events of the day, she practically passed out. Safe in their arms, she slept.

At least for a few hours.

10

Later that night, Jace's phone buzzed. The three of them roused, on high alert. He rolled out of bed naked and wandered into the living room. His voice waxed and waned as he spoke, as if he was pacing the impressive length of the windows overlooking the city.

"Must be our captain." Ian stifled a yawn with his loosely curved fist. "Wish Jace had more to tell him. There's something else here, I know it."

"Where will you look next?" she wondered, though she knew the answer before she overheard Jace request ladders, saws, and snake cameras to be delivered the next day.

"The ceiling." Ian drew her over him so she was sprawled on top of his broad chest. He rubbed her back and said, "The guy was planning to use the utility conduits, so we know he had access. It's the only logical place we haven't turned over today."

"I know you have to, but...ugh." Casey dropped her forehead to his shoulder, resigned. Things were going to get a hell of a lot messier.

With the investigation, and likely with her love life.

To take her mind off the discussion going on outside the bedroom walls, she turned her focus on Ian. For a man she hadn't met until yesterday, she felt oddly at ease with him.

So comfortable, in fact, she started asking questions that might have been better left unasked. "I get why Jace is into this arrangement. The insurance you give him. But what about you? Why do you like teaming up with him to fuck women? What do you get out of it besides playing babysitter?"

"While he and I might have spent our time together before hooking up with you letting off steam through sex, I'd prefer if you didn't consider what's happening here something as simple as a quick double-team. For Jace, this is like two percent about sex and ninety-eight percent about rekindling a meaningful relationship with you. I hope you don't take that lightly. It could crush him." He lifted her chin so she could look into his eyes when he said, "I understand why he's so invested in you. You're special. Someone we could last a lifetime with, I think."

Oh. It sounded nice. Made her warm and gooey inside to hear it. Casey didn't doubt Ian meant it either. She just wasn't sure it was possible to make such grand statements after a handful of orgasms and a single completely abnormal day spent together.

"We're practically strangers, Ian." She kissed him gently then, hoping he didn't take offense to her frankness. "How can you even suspect something that monumental?"

He shrugged. "Because Jace believes it. He knows me. He knows you. If he thinks it's the right fit, I trust him."

Casey tried not to be irrationally offended that he

didn't profess love at first sight. Though it affronted her pride, it appeased her brain, which kept insisting this was crazy.

"Don't mistake what I'm saying." He placated her with a longer, deeper kiss. "You're obviously gorgeous; it only takes a moment to see that. We're clearly compatible in bed. The rest takes time. Time I'm willing to devote my energy to in order to make this partnership work. For all three of us. It's pretty much the only chance I have to be happy."

"But you really never answered my question about why you want this. You're handsome, generous, and intelligent. What woman wouldn't want you?"

"I'm not sure I can explain. My whole life, I've enjoyed taking care of people. Looking out for them. It's one of the main reasons it was my goal to be a cop for as long as I can remember. I looked after my grandmother, too. I used to stop in every day after school, and when she got to the point that she either needed live-in care or would have had to leave her home for a nursing facility, my parents agreed I should move in with her. I was seventeen. I'm grateful for the time I spent with her those last few years. When she was gone, though, I felt useless."

Casey hugged him tight. Though her mom hadn't been perfect, it had still hurt when she'd gotten the news that she was gone. She couldn't imagine the pain of losing someone you were that close to.

For a few minutes he was quiet, reflecting. Eventually he continued, "I had a girlfriend not too long after that, who asked me to be adventurous and invite a guy I knew from school to join us for a one-time thing. It only took that one time for me to be hooked on doubling the pleasure I can give my partner, on being able to sit back and watch them unravel." He hummed. "It's a more potent high than anything else I've experienced."

"So what happened to your girlfriend?" Casey wondered.

"Eh. Turns out she really wanted the other guy instead of me and was looking for a convenient trial run before dumping my ass." He shook his head as he grinned. "It's okay, though. We're still friends. We got along fine, but... there was always something missing. That lightning I can see flashing between you and Jace the instant you're in the same room together. That's what I've been looking for."

He closed his eyes, though not before she saw the sadness there. She hated the way it looked on him, especially after he'd done so much to care for her on one of the best and worst days of her life.

"Hey, what's that about?" She rubbed light circles on his chest and waited patiently for him to trust her. Or not.

"I'm tired of hooking up with people I don't care about. I think it's easier for Jace to separate physical satisfaction from his emotions. He's been doing it for a decade. For me, it's not that simple. I give a piece of my heart to every woman we're with. Yet we always end up walking away...sooner rather than later. It's making this hole inside me that gets bigger and bigger every time. I'm not sure how much more I can take."

She fell a little bit in love with him right then, she was pretty sure.

"I'm worried we can't keep going like we have been. Jace can sense it too. We've been going out less and less as it is. Now that he's had you again, he'll never settle for anything less. Whether he admits it or not, Jace needs to be loved. Those old scars haven't fully healed over. You might be the only person who can salve those wounds and make him whole. For that, I'm willing to take a chance." He ran his hand along her side. "And the more I get to know you, the more I'm thinking it's less risky than I'd imagined even yesterday."

"Thanks, Ian." She kissed him then, sweetly with a hint of spice. "I'm feeling pretty good about things myself. Though I sort of liked fucking a stranger. That was a fun game."

"It can be even better when you sleep with someone who understands every inch of you and all the mental quirks that will push you to extreme heights. Will you consider turning this one-night stand into something more meaningful? A real relationship?" He paused. "That's all I'm asking, that you give this a shot."

"I'm not sure, Ian. Can't we see where things take us? I'm afraid, too—of getting burned again. The longer I spend with you two, the more likely I am to end up hurt. It's a lot to ask after just one day."

"I know, I'm sorry. I shouldn't have said anything." He rubbed his eyes with his knuckles.

"I asked, you answered." Casey smiled at him. "I'm not a lawyer for nothing."

Ian chuckled. "I bet you're spectacular at your job."

"I am."

Jace leaned against the doorjamb, his ankles crossed. "Are you two having fun without me?"

"I'm too tired for more *fun*," she answered honestly.

"It's been a hell of a day," he agreed as he wandered closer then sank into bed.

Sandwiched between Ian and Jace, she couldn't have felt safer. Or sleepier.

"We've got you," Ian promised.

"Yes, you do." She hoped he realized she was talking about more than their imminent snugglefest.

The guys wrapped around her, cocooning her in their strong limbs and heat. She was asleep before anyone could say another word.

11

Casey woke the next morning when sunlight speared through the enormous windows of her bedroom, directly into her face. Ugh. Good thing she got up before the sun most days.

When she could stop squinting long enough to bring her bedroom into focus, the first thing she saw was Jace's handsome face. It was so rare to catch him like that—relaxed, resting—that she took her time memorizing the mask of serenity he wore in sleep.

"You really knocked him out," Ian murmured from behind her.

She jumped. Oops. Busted drooling over her ex-boyfriend. Or were they dating again? She should probably clarify that at some point.

Ian chuckled. "Forget about me so soon?"

"Of course not." She grinned. "It'd be impossible not to notice something that big jabbing me in the ass."

"Anal play is Jace's specialty, not mine." He nuzzled the nape of her neck before kissing lightly beneath her ear, making her shiver.

"Did somebody say anal?" Jace mumbled, then scrubbed his face with his hands and stretched. He turned to face them with a wicked grin.

Casey snickered. "Figures that would rouse you."

"It's your fucking fault I'm obsessed with the back door." He wrapped his arm around her hip then rolled her onto her stomach so he could swat her cheeks, massage them, then trace the valley between them with the tip of one finger. "The time we tried it still stands as one of the best nights of my life. It was intense to share that first with you."

It had been, though she wasn't sure she wanted to admit it.

"Hey, I'll try anything once." She shrugged one shoulder. Her legs shifted restlessly against the sheets, a desperate attempt to quell the arousal bubbling up within her. "That doesn't mean I want to do it every day or ever again, for that matter."

"Is that a general comment, or are you bored with ménage already?" Ian asked, sounding legitimately concerned.

Before she could reassure him, Jace pled their case. "We have some other kinky tricks up our sleeves...or down our pants, however that saying goes."

"Hmm..." She decided to string them along. "You know, I'm an experienced woman now. You're going to have to work hard to keep it interesting."

"Well, ma'am, I'm an officer of the law and I think I'm about to arrest you for being far too fucking hot for two ordinary men." Ian reached over to his nightstand and returned dangling a set of handcuffs from his index finger.

"You're right. I've been a bad girl." Casey had been shocked the first time Jace had restrained her. Shocked and inexplicably turned on. It seemed not much had changed since then. She hadn't realized it because she'd never trusted anyone else enough to allow them to bind her. "You'd better make sure I can't escape, then show me what you're capable of."

Jace pounced. He flipped her over and had her wrists pinned in one of his hands before she could even pretend to fight him. Truth was, she was already caught. By them.

It would have been impossible for her to get up and leave when they were looking at her like they were about to treat her to the best morning sex of her life. She squirmed. Nope, not getting loose.

To erase any lingering doubt, Jace nodded at Ian, who fastened one of the cuffs around her wrist before feeding the chain through one of the metal swirls of her headboard. Then he snapped the other around her second wrist.

The click of the chain against her bed inspired a shiver. The good kind.

Instinctively, she spread her legs, hoping one of the men would accept her invitation.

"Not so fast, babe." Jace ran his hand from her knee to her crotch.

She moaned. He cupped her pussy, teasing her as much with his touches as he did with what he told her next.

"You said yourself, you're an expert in ménage." Jace leaned in and nipped her bottom lip. "So it shouldn't be any problem for you to fuck us both at once."

She tugged on the cuffs then. No luck. No breaking free.

"Do you think you're up for that?" Ian asked her softly,

making sure she wasn't truly trying to run from them, while Jace maintained his roleplay character.

She nodded emphatically. Jace smiled down at her, rewarding her with a brush of his thumb over her clit. Fuck. Casey arched toward his touch, so he did it again. It wouldn't be long before things progressed from playing to full-on fucking.

"Do you have any lube?" Ian asked. Thank God he was thinking of practicalities. She and Jace certainly weren't.

She'd personally moved in her toy chest and put it in the closet to avoid any accidents. The last thing she needed was for the movers to have dropped it on the lobby floor and spilled her vibrators, accessories, and decent-sized gay porn collection in front of the doorman, Lenny.

If that had happened, she would have had to move right back out again...if she hadn't died of embarrassment first.

"Casey?" Ian repeated.

"Yeah. It's in the black steamer trunk in the closet." She was either going to regret telling him that or it was going to lead to one of the more amazing moments of her life. She hoped for the latter. "There are condoms in there, too."

"Good, I used my wallet stash last night," Jace admitted. "Hustle, Ian."

While Ian gathered supplies, Jace rocked her onto her side again, facing away from him this time. He wrapped her in his arms and squeezed. Though he didn't say anything, she knew he was trying to tell her how grateful he was to have her again, if only for however long this lasted.

She knew because she felt the same way.

Then his hands began to roam from her breasts over her stomach to her pussy. He took his time, turning her on, making every part of her body hum with appreciation. When Ian came back, he took a moment to appreciate the sight of them together.

"Damn, that's sexy." His stare raked the length of her bound, stretched body.

"We're lucky bastards, aren't we?" Jace asked him.

"Hell yeah." Ian nodded, then dropped his hand to his cock so he could stroke himself fully hard and roll on a condom. Casey licked her lips as she watched the liquid grace of his movements. He'd fucked like that, too. Smooth. She couldn't wait to feel him sliding within her again.

"Come over here and distract her while I get her ready," Jace ordered Ian.

He did as he was told, as he clearly wanted to do anyway. When he sank to the bed before her, he handed Jace a condom and lube along with a hard plastic vibrator. One of the basic ones she'd gotten a long time ago before she'd known about rabbit vibrators or more realistic materials. It was a lot thinner and more tapered than most of her other toys.

"This will work." Jace hummed from behind her. She could feel the bed move as he too put on protection and investigated the tools Ian had scavenged for him to use on her.

Then Casey lost track of exactly what Jace was up to, because Ian began to kiss her.

Damn, he was so good at it. He made her hornier than she could have imagined just with his lips and mouth and wandering hands.

"Get inside. Distract her while I get her ready," Jace

said softly, as though trying not to tear her from the daze Ian was putting her into. She closed her eyes and focused on the pressure of her cuffed hands, Ian's mouth, and the nudge of his cock between her legs.

Jace took her top knee in his palm and lifted it, easing the way for his partner to penetrate her. Ian didn't hesitate —he began to work his shaft into her while he made out with her, bringing them together with grinds of his pelvis that wedged him inside her bit by bit. He didn't drive into her with long, hurried thrusts. No, he fucked her with measured presses of his hips that flexed his ass beneath her heel. When had she wrapped that leg around him? Maybe Jace had put it there.

He seemed busy with something else behind her, but she wasn't about to take her attention from the wonderful things Ian was doing to her to find out.

"You feel incredible hugging me like that," Ian whispered to her between kisses. "Your pussy is so hot and slick around me. I could fuck you forever."

"Good. Keep going." She rocked her hips to meet him when he ground deep within her.

With her arms bound, it was the only way she could reach out to him. The thrill of being captive between them escalated her arousal. She didn't think it could get much better until she felt the press of something cool and hard behind her.

Casey moaned. She didn't have a chance to do more than that before Jace inserted the tip of the toy in her ass. Even that felt enormous. She hadn't had anything inside her back there since he'd left.

"Relax," Ian whispered. "It will feel better if you don't fight us."

He redoubled his efforts at making her crazy with lust.

It was effective.

The zings of discomfort faded as her body accommodated the smallest part of her vibrator. Jace must have felt it because he began sliding it in deeper. She appreciated the warm up considering his cock was as thick and stocky as he was.

She had a glimpse of what it would be like when they were both inside her, and she groaned. Ian murmured encouragement and increased the swing of his hips. He fucked her so well, she thought she might come too soon and ruin their fun.

Just when she thought it couldn't get much better, Jace switched on the vibrator.

Casey shouted his name. She clamped down on Ian and the toy. There wasn't any conscious choice, or time to warn them, or ask permission to change their little game.

She couldn't resist this much stimulation. She came hard around Ian.

He groaned and fucked through her spasms, working harder to plunge through her rippling channel of muscles. To her surprise, though, he didn't join her. When she could breathe again, she opened her eyes and saw the concentration etched into his.

Jace said, "Damn, babe. You're even more responsive than I remembered. Even sexier. You're so beautiful when you come."

She could only shiver, still experiencing aftershocks of pleasure that were being reborn into an even stronger desire.

"Come on, Jace." Ian rasped. "Quit fucking around. I'm not going to last if she comes again. And I want her to feel us together."

Casey wanted that too. Needed it.

She arched her spine so that her ass jutted out toward Jace.

He took the bait.

Despite the toy, which had been removed sometime while she was incapacitated with bliss, he didn't ease inside her ass. He lodged his fat tip at the entrance to her body then pressed, but he didn't get far. A sharp pain had her gasping and tensing in Ian's arms, though not for the right reasons.

"More lube, Jace." Ian was watching out for her, even as he kept her riding the high of her orgasm, which had extended into more passion.

The weight of Jace's cock disappeared. His fingers, slick with lubrication, probed her back entrance, making her moan and squirm with the dual sensation of his fingering and Ian's fucking.

She might die next time she came.

Before long, his cock was back. It glided through her crack until it notched in her asshole.

This time, when he advanced, Ian kissed her softly. She sighed and gave herself to them completely. Jace grunted as he sank into her body.

Casey melted. With her arms held fast above her head and the guys skewering her from both sides, she couldn't do much but lie there and take it. Didn't want to do anything else except enjoy their attention, either.

Rational thought evaporated. All she could do was feel. And enjoy.

The pressure of both of them inside her, invading her simultaneously, nearly tore her apart in the most pleasant way possible. They filled her completely—with their cocks and emotions she wasn't sure she was ready to handle.

So she brushed her feelings aside in favor of pure rapture.

The guys moved within her, sometimes in sync, sometimes in counterpoint. They told her with their groans and curses how good it felt for them, too.

She imagined that they could feel each other's cocks stroking their own through the thin walls of her body that separated them.

Jace gripped her hip and plunged deeper, making them all cry out together. "Rub her clit, Ian. Get her off. Take us down with her."

Casey tipped her head back, desperate to kiss him. He obliged before Ian reclaimed her mouth. The men took turns feasting on her lips as they rode her. And when Ian slipped his hand between them and drew circles around her clit while they pumped into her, she gathered around them.

Everything within her got tighter and tighter and tighter until finally it released in the big bang of all orgasms. The instant her body began milking them, Ian and Jace came, too. Their simultaneous releases only made her orgasm stronger. Longer.

She flew, soaring on endorphins and the affection of the two men beside her, inside her.

It was a long time before she felt first Jace and then Ian slip free of her body.

They flanked her, catching their breath as all three of them recovered from orgasms powerful enough to impact all of their lives. Hopefully for the better.

She sagged, putting tension on her shoulder since she was still shackled to her own bed. Right then, she prayed they never let her go.

12

Casey snuggled between Ian and Jace. If her hands hadn't started going numb, she could easily have taken a nap despite never having gotten out of bed that morning. Even if she stayed awake, just lying between them and dreaming about the possibilities would be as restorative as the best night's sleep.

Her stomach growled.

"Want me to bring you breakfast in bed?" Ian asked.

She changed her mind. The whitewashed wooden tray piled high with pancakes, eggs, bacon, and one of the bud vases she collected with a rose in it sounded a heck of a lot better than dropping back into unconsciousness.

"Please." She arched against him. "I'll even tip you with a blowjob."

"I could learn to cook for a blowjob," Jace grunted.

"Pouring junk cereal into a bowl does not count as cooking." Ian shoved Jace's shoulder, then rolled to the edge of the bed. "I'd rather not die of food poisoning now that I have a reason to hang around, either."

They all paused as his comment sank in. He tried to blow it off as a joke, but neither Casey nor Jace believed he wasn't serious, based on the look they exchanged.

"While he's taking care of us, could you let me go?" Casey looked up at Jace. "I'm starting to lose feeling in my fingers."

"Shit. Sorry." He rolled to his side and reached for the key on the night table.

Except just then, an odd scuffling sound came from the ceiling.

Casey might have assumed it was some of NYC's famous rats if she still lived in her old apartment. Here, though, not likely. Besides, that would have to be one hell of a giant rat.

"Motherfucker!" Jace whisper-shouted as he diverted his hand from the key to the cuffs to his gun, which sat beside it.

As Casey stared, a thin black line appeared on the ceiling. The crack grew, shooting out like a lightning bolt in the summer sky. Then a chunk of plaster fell. Ian put one hand on her hip and rocked her so that it at least landed on her hip and not on the softly rounded curves of her belly.

It still hurt, though not as much as the miscellaneous elbows and knees that followed when a man, who was definitely bigger than a rodent, dropped from the sky.

He bounced off the bed in a tuck-and-roll worthy of an acrobat in the Ringling Brothers Circus.

Before Casey could even truly register what was happening, Jace was pulling his gun out of the holster, while Ian positioned himself between her nude body and the intruder.

Hell, none of them even had clothes on. Talk about

getting caught with your pants down. She was fucking cuffed by the good guys!

This was going to be bad.

Jace took a split second to check on her and Ian, the slightest turn of his head, his protective instinct kicking in. And that's all it took.

The newcomer kicked out and smashed his booted foot into Jace's fist. The gun went flying.

Both Jace and the other guy flung themselves at it like a pair of football players scrambling for a loose ball. They tumbled around on the floor, smashing her full-length mirror and nearly toppling a dresser in the process. Ian gripped her legs, still acting as a human shield in case the worst happened.

It did.

Jace roared as the desperate criminal resorted to biting Jace's arm while they grappled. The guy took advantage of the temporary loss of motion in Jace's arm and emerged from their tussle holding Jace's gun.

Ian leaned forward, prepared to take up the fight.

"If you come one step closer, I'll blow his head off!" the intruder roared at Ian while pointing the gun at Jace. "Then I'll take care of your lady friend here and save you for last. Maybe I'll make you watch me fuck her first, since you've tied her up for me. It seems she's the kind of bitch that'll fuck anyone based on all that racket you were making. I appreciate it. If the fucking floor hadn't given out, I'd have taken off before you even realized I was here. Stupid fucking cops."

He spit on the floor then pointed the gun directly at Jace's face.

"No! Don't hurt him!" Casey screamed. How would she live the rest of her life after watching his brains splatter all over her dove-gray walls and the white carpet of her perfect penthouse? She couldn't survive it. Couldn't stand for him to be stolen from the world now that she'd just rediscovered him and their undying connection.

In that moment she knew, unequivocally, that she loved Jace West.

Always had and always would.

He glanced over his shoulder at her and Ian. The look he gave them said everything she'd ever needed to hear from him. Pure adoration radiated from him in that moment.

Jace was resigned to his fate.

Except right then a bang sounded from down the hall.

Not a gunshot.

It sounded more like the front door smashing into the wall after being kicked in.

A moment later, Gabriel's voice rang out, ordering Goliath, "Go, boy! Find them, get 'em. Go!"

Their savior must have heard her screams on the way to their morning walk.

After playing with the friendly if oversized pup, she never would have imagined he could transform into the vicious, snarling freight train of terror that barreled into the room a few seconds later.

His head whipped toward her, then to Jace, who whistled. "Goliath, here."

The animal must have sensed the aggression in their intruder. He didn't hesitate. He barked furiously as he leapt. His weight crashed into the guy holding a gun on Jace, causing enough distraction to allow Jace to duck just as the man pulled the trigger.

Goliath yelped and fell to the floor along with Jace.

Ian shouted for his partner and joined the fray. He

bashed the intruder in the face with his elbow, dazing him long enough that Jace was able to wrestle the gun from his hand and turn it on him. Jace trembled with a rage Casey hadn't seen in him since he was young and powerless to help the women his father attacked.

"Jace, no!" she screeched, trying to drag herself closer to him. With her wrists bound and completely numb, it was futile.

Casey shouldn't have worried. Ian was there. He wouldn't let Jace do anything that would land him in trouble. He wrapped his fingers around Jace's wrist and spoke softly, calmly. "It's over. Backup will be here in a few minutes. Don't do it, Jace."

From the doorway, Casey heard Gabriel praying through his tears as he looked at the blood pooling on the floor beneath Goliath, who'd gone still.

"Is he...?" Casey couldn't even say it. She felt sick.

Ian watched Jace, while Jace watched the man responsible for this nightmare.

Gabriel ran to Goliath. He whipped off his shirt, wrapped it around him, high on his front left leg, then cradled the dog in his arms. "I think I can feel a pulse. A faint one. He needs a vet. I can't wait. Everly went to call 911."

"Take him," Ian said without once shifting his focus off Jace.

Gabriel lifted the dog and staggered out, the rest of them be damned. Casey didn't blame him one bit.

"You might as well shoot me," the burglar taunted Jace, trying to get him to do it. "I'm a dead man in prison. I know too much. You know the boss will have me killed before the first night is over. At least this will be over before I know it."

Ian stepped in then. "Or you could help us out. Tell us everything you know and put a stop to it. Our captain will cut a deal with you, protect you."

The man scoffed, but he didn't seem entirely committed to his disdain.

"You're right. You don't have a very long life expectancy in prison. Think about it." Ian morphed into cop mode before her eyes. He was persuasive as fuck.

The guy didn't respond. He gave Ian a barely perceptible nod, though. With a key witness like this scumbag, they were going to have all the testimony they needed to put the kingpin away for good. "They sent me to check around for anything that had been left behind. There's at least a million dollars stashed in bundles up there and I know where the body is."

"Which body?" Jace asked.

"The one of the guy who used to live here."

At least this had all been worth it.

13

Casey admitted it. She was hiding.

After tolerating what seemed like endless questioning, which she generally understood the need for from her law classes—even if she wasn't a criminal attorney—but definitely did not appreciate, she slunk off to her master bathroom.

She'd dumped an entire box of bath bombs into the claw-foot tub overlooking the Manhattan skyline, filled that fucker full of steaming hot water, and climbed inside, hoping to scrub away some of the lingering terror and hopelessness that would haunt her for a good long while.

The mirrored film on the window allowed her to see out without giving anyone with binoculars or a telescope a show. She studied the patterns of the traffic on the grid of streets and the frantic pace of life most of New Yorkers reveled in.

Casey was one of them. Or had been.

What had happened earlier, nearly losing her own life or those of her loved ones, had her rethinking a few things. She wasn't ever going to be happy being idle. But maybe there was a middle ground. If the guys agreed with her, she hoped they could explore it together.

A soft knock came on the door. "Are you decent?" Jace asked.

"No. But you should come in anyway."

He poked his head around the door. "Damn."

Jace came inside and closed the door. Either because there were still people out there, documenting the crime scene, cleaning the blood out of her rug, and conducting interviews with Ian. Or because he realized she wanted to keep the steam inside where it filled her lungs with warmth and the soothing scent of essential oils.

He stared at her.

"What?" Casey lifted her hands, cupping her breasts and shielding herself from his scrutiny.

"Sometimes it's hard for me to see the girl I used to love inside all this fancy wrapping." Jace sat on the edge of the bathtub and swiped the washcloth from her hand.

"I'm still the same person, but better. Why can't I be both?" She blinked up at him, damp lashes probably looking even darker on her pale skin when they clumped together. Hopefully he didn't mistake her temporary need to recover for weakness. "Is it so bad, to enjoy these things I've worked hard for?"

"That's not what I'm trying to say." He ran the soft linen across her skin reverently. "It's just like going to a museum or something. Like I should look, but not touch. Like I'm some common slob staring at a masterpiece."

"I like it when you touch," she admitted in a sultry murmur. "Maybe this will jog your memory. Do you remember that summer I talked you into manning the dunk tank at the school fundraiser?"

"The summer you were also the high school's star

softball pitcher?" Jace shook his head, laughing. "Uh huh, sure do."

Casey wrapped her fingers around his wrist and yanked, sending him tumbling into the sudsy water. Sputtering, he surfaced, slinging water everywhere with a shake of his head. "What the—?"

Ian burst through the door then, gun drawn. "Is everything okay?"

"She's lost her fucking mind." Jace stared at Casey with huge eyes. "And now I made a mess."

Oh no, that wouldn't do. Casey lunged forward and wrapped her arms around his neck, plastering their soaked bodies together. "Just because I can afford nice things doesn't mean I don't like to get down and dirty. And if you think for one damn minute that you're not good enough for me, I'm going to dunk you again until you listen to what I'm saying. If you freak out and leave me right now, when we've only just found each other again, I'm not sure if I'll be able to get over it. If you want to be with me— both of you—now that you don't *have* to stay, it's going to be important not to trigger my fear of losing you again. Especially after what could have happened today."

Ian chuckled from the doorway. "Maybe he'll believe it considering you've said exactly what I told him a minute ago."

"See, Jace, Ian's so smart. You should listen to him." She kissed him then so he knew she thought he was plenty amazing, too.

When they finally broke apart, he said, "I'm taking you to bed before someone slips and knocks themselves unconscious. We work with the paramedics too often to have to call in something like that. We'd never hear the end of it."

"Here, let me dry her off before you mess up her pretty sheets." Ian whipped a towel off the heated rack and held his arms open. Jace lifted her from the sudsy water and offered her to his partner. They really were like a two-man machine, working in tandem.

Ian collected her from Jace, then set her on the bathmat. He paid special attention to her breasts and between her legs while Jace shed his own sopping clothes then hurriedly swiped a towel across his stunning body. Casey promised herself she'd take time to explore every single inch of it with her tongue at some point soon.

"I think she's dry enough," Jace growled.

Dropping the towel, Ian followed the same trail he'd brushed the terrycloth over with his fingers. He hummed and stole a kiss. When he lifted his head to look at Jace, who didn't seem to mind too much, he said, "Wrong again, my friend. She's plenty wet."

Jace cursed, then scooped her up and hoisted her over his shoulder. Her bare ass stuck into the air as he strode into her bedroom and tossed her on the bed. Casey squeaked as she bounced.

It took her a moment to realize the curtains were still drawn, thanks to the circling news choppers. The soft, warm light flickering around them came from at least a hundred different tea light candles scattered around the room. Flower petals dotted the spaces between them. She knew Ian was responsible for the intimate setting.

"I take it this means everyone's gone and the place is locked up?" Jace asked.

Ian nodded.

"How did you pull this off?" Casey asked, touched that

he'd bothered, even knowing he was going to get lucky regardless.

"Everly had some supplies leftover from a reception on the rooftop deck." He shrugged as if it was no big deal that he'd gone to the trouble of asking her and making sure what might be their last time together was perfect.

As if by tacit understanding, the guys shifted gears from the animalistic claiming they'd staked previously to something softer, more romantic, and sincere. Something she'd have a hell of a hard time resisting. Afraid to ask if this meant they were looking for more than a few quick fucks, Casey decided to enjoy their time together before ruining it with worries.

"Ian's going to fuck you," Jace told her as he sat near her head and rested her face on his thigh. "I want your mouth on me while I watch. I love to see you enjoying yourself."

"You never were one to turn down a blowjob, either," she joked.

Ian spanked her then, surprising her. "He's not joking. It means a lot to him to see you happy, you know?"

Casey nodded. "Same for me."

"Good." Ian smiled and put her in position. She was lying on her back, her head still on Jace's thigh. He cradled her head in his hands and directed her mouth where he wanted it.

She licked him first, remembering the musky taste of his flesh and how turned on she got using her mouth to unravel him. Jace, her strong, protective boyfriend, could be easily undone with attention from her tongue and lips in just the right places. Casey did her best to drive him wild.

In the meantime, Ian began to do the same to her. He

put on a condom then settled over her. The weight of his full contact was nearly as good as the handcuffs had been earlier. She felt secure, surrounded, maybe even loved.

He eased inside her and began to make lazy love to her. No hurry this time.

They wanted it to last. So did she, afraid that this might be a farewell fuck.

For longer than she could keep track of, they took care of each other's needs, indulged each other in a competition to see who could give the most pleasure.

She sucked on Jace's cock, softly at first, treating him to gentle licks and hums. Only after she began to taste his precome did she begin to escalate her attentions. Around that time, Ian also cracked, beginning to pump inside her a little faster and harder.

It was the most decadent sex of her life. And also some of the most meaningful. Because it became about what each of them could give instead of what they were receiving in return.

When a moan slipped from her, the guys responded in turn.

Finally it was too much. She began to clench around Ian.

"It's time," he told Jace.

Jace smiled down at her. "I love you, Casey. I always have. I'd do anything to give you this feeling forever."

It was as if he'd found a secret G-spot in the region of her heart. Casey responded in the only way possible. She came, shuddering between Jace and Ian. Her climax wrecked them, drawing the come from Ian's balls as surely as her moans around Jace's shaft triggered his orgasm as well. He shot pulse after pulse of seed down her throat.

Greedily, she drank it, eager to have any part of him he'd share.

Ian groaned, locked himself as deep as possible within her, then collapsed on top of her. She reveled in the weight of him, pressing her to the mattress.

Eventually he rolled, taking her with him so she lay on his chest. Jace stretched out beside them, putting a protective arm across her back. She took turns kissing each man until they succumbed to exhaustion.

14

_____

It was late afternoon before they roused from another round of spectacular sex. Jace untangled himself from her and Ian reluctantly followed suit, letting her go from his embrace. Was this where things got awkward?

"Well, I guess we should head home and let you get a good night's sleep since you're going back to work tomorrow." He brushed a few stray strands of hair away from her eyes, then kissed her forehead softly and sweetly. "I know you're going to want to be on top of your game."

Didn't he understand that she'd sleep far better with him and Ian here than when she was alone? "Why don't you guys stay?"

"Like for the night?" Ian asked.

"Or however long this lasts. Maybe a lot longer..." She was afraid to over commit or frighten them away. They were notorious bachelors, after all.

Speaking for herself, she couldn't imagine ever growing tired of their special brand of loving or how they satisfied both the base and sophisticated facets of her personality.

"What will you do when people talk?" Jace asked.

"Living with us, having an unconventional relationship, could jeopardize your career." Ian frowned. "We wouldn't ever do something that would hurt you."

"Oh no, not this again." Casey shook her head vehemently, grinning inwardly when their gazes locked on her jiggling tits. "I've learned my lesson the hard way. My happiness is more important than what people think of me. If anyone objects to my personal choices or my lifestyle, they can fuck off. I'm still one of the best at what I do. If my place in the company deteriorates, I can always start my own practice and become their competition."

"So...are you asking us to move in?" Jace asked.

"This penthouse—and my bed—are plenty big enough for three. Just saying." She nibbled her lower lip. Each second that passed seemed to take as long as one of her bar exams. "There are even enough rooms for you each to have your own if you're not sure about sharing the same space right away. Or I could sell it if you prefer Ian's townhouse. Not that I'm inviting myself or anything."

"Maybe we'd better test your bed out again, so we can compare it to Ian's place." Jace winked at her before tackling her to the rumpled sheets. She shrieked as he and Ian ganged up to tickle her ribs.

At that, a deep bark echoed off the walls and windows of her room.

"It's okay, Goliath. Don't get up. I'm fine. They're just playing." Casey hopped off the bed and sat on the floor next to the ginormous doggy bed—which was really more like a doggie palace—they'd set up for her new favorite neighbor. While Gabriel was out volunteering, she kept an eye on his faithful companion. It was the least she could do since they'd risked their lives for her, Ian, and Jace.

The vet had said it would take a few weeks for him to heal completely after the procedures they'd done to repair his shoulder. Until then, he was being treated like a king. They'd offered to pay the bills of the fancy in-home vet that allowed him to avoid staying in the pet hospital for long.

The big brown dog laid his head on her thigh and stared up at her with wide mopey eyes until she caved and cracked open his treat jug. He snarfled the handful of nuggets in her palm before she could even properly hold them out to him.

"He has you wrapped around his tail." Jace shook his head, though he patted Goliath too. Ian joined in with a few *good doggy*s.

"I know how he feels." She grinned up at the two men flanking her.

"Just imagine how much worse it would be if he was a baby instead of a dog," Ian said to Jace.

Jace blanched. "Uh...is that something you would like?"

Did he think that children might be a reason for them to fall apart again? As far as Casey was concerned, the world needed more love, in whatever form it took. "Why not? You and I know that when a child is starved for attention and affection, bad things happen. With three people to split the responsibilities and lavish them with love, how could that hurt?"

They'd always talked about having a proper family, one where they could right the wrongs they'd endured, so she didn't think he'd take off if she admitted she could envision kids filling up those other bedrooms. You know, not today or tomorrow...but it was a possibility for someday.

"I'll be back in a bit." Jace spun on his heel and strode from the room. "Ian, come on."

"Where are you two going?" she called. Hadn't she convinced them?

"Gotta pack enough to stay until we figure out where we should live for good."

Casey threw her head back and laughed. She hugged herself as she rested against the warm glass and ran her hand over and over Goliath's fur.

Now she truly had it all—a successful career, a couple of people who could become close friends, two men who made her taboo fantasies come true, and a future she couldn't wait to share with them.

Moving to Beekman Place had been the best decision of her life.

MORE PENTHOUSE PLEASURES

COMING SOON!

Check out the rest of the Penthouse Pleasures books for five more stories about Casey's neighbors.

Voyeur - August 2017
Daddy - September 2017
Sinner - October 2017
Fetish - November 2017
Bound - December 2017

EXCERPT FROM DADDY

PENTHOUSE PLEASURES #3

Kent stepped into the police station and walked to the desk.

"I'm Kent Grayson. I was called about a young woman named Christina Mills."

"Oh, yeah," the sergeant said. "Detective Rosco wants to talk to you. He'll be right out."

Kent paced. He wasn't used to being kept waiting, and ordinarily he'd have one of his staff handle this sort of thing. Not that this exact sort of thing had ever happened before. He didn't usually consort with the type of person who got picked up by the police in the middle of the night.

But Christina was the daughter of an old friend and she was in trouble.

"Mr. Grayson."

Kent looked up to see a man in torn jeans and a leather jacket, full beard walking toward him.

"I'm Detective Rosco," he said as he held out his hand and Kent shook it. "I understand you're Ms. Mills stepfather."

Kent didn't allow the shock of that statement to affect his expression.

"Where is Christina? Is she all right?"

He couldn't help remembering the last time he saw Christina. Her long blonde hair swept back from her face, held by a clip at the back of her head. Her heart-shaped lips turned up in a smile that set her innocent face aglow. It had been her sixteenth birthday and he'd come to visit so he could give her a special gift.

She'd always been fascinated by the fact he lived in New York City. She'd loved the idea of living somewhere as exciting as New York. It was all she'd ever talked about. So he'd given her a necklace with the I Love NY logo in gold. When she'd opened it, her eyes had gone wide and she'd thrown her arms around him.

"She's fine." The detective led Kent through a door, then down a hallway. "But she's gotten herself into some trouble. That's why I wanted to have a talk with you."

As they walked, Kent saw several women sitting on a bench in a waiting room. Hookers by the look of them in their skimpy, suggestive clothing. One young woman's gaze locked on him and she stood up.

Fuck, she was stunning, despite the slutty dress she wore. Her hair cascaded over her shoulders in sunny waves and the tight dress that hugged her perfect body was cut low in front, showing the generous swell of her creamy breasts. And it was so short it showed every inch of her long, shapely legs.

She surged toward him.

"Daddy," she cried as she threw her arms around him.

What the fuck?

Then he realized. *This* was Christina.

"Please," she whispered desperately against his ear. "I told them you're my stepfather. Please go along with it."

Fuck, he could barely think straight. She was clearly distraught and he'd wrapped his arms around her in an automatic need to comfort her, but his body tightened at the feel of her breasts pushed tight against him. Making him want things he shouldn't want. Tickling a need buried so deep inside him, he dared not let it loose.

He grasped her shoulders and eased her back, then gazed into her shimmering green eyes.

"Christina, what's going on?"

"I'm sorry, Daddy. It's not as bad as what they're going to tell you."

He narrowed his eyes. One, he wished she'd stopped calling him Daddy because... damn it... it was seriously messing with his head. Two, how the hell had the sweet young girl he'd known become... a prostitute?

"Sit down, Ms. Mills," Detective Rosco said to her. "Mr. Grayson, let's talk."

He led Kent to a room with a table and closed the door.

"She told us you're her stepfather but that you and her mother are separated. She didn't know how to get in touch with you."

"I haven't seen her or her mother for several years. So what is she being charged with?"

"We picked her up outside a bar for soliciting. We have one witness. The guy we caught talking to her. He said she came on to him, offering to go back to his hotel room for money."

Detective Rosco leaned back in his chair.

"She has no priors, but she also has no permanent address and no job." He leaned forward. "I know this must be disturbing for you. I just want to say that I've seen a lot of young woman on the street but whatever's going on with her isn't that bad. Yet."

The thought of Christina fucking men for money seemed pretty bad to Kent. In fact, the thought ate away at his gut, making him feel sick.

The detective leaned forward, looking Kent square in the eyes.

"I think there's still time to straighten her out and get her back on the right track. *If* you're willing to get involved. I could put her in jail, but I'd rather turn her over to you. If you'll agree to give her the time and effort to try and turn her around."

"And what do you have in mind?"

"I'd like you to agree to keep her with you for no less than a month. Spend time with her. Show her you care. Maybe she just needs some stability."

"I can do that."

"Good. I'm glad to hear that."

WANT MORE STEAMY MENAGE ROMANCES?

If you've enjoyed Taboo, check out another of Jayne's menage romance series Powertools and the related series Hot Rods. Powertools kicks off with Kate's Crew. Read it by clicking here.

Nothing's sexier than men with power tools.

Sultry summer heat has nothing on the five-man crew renovating the house next door. No one could blame Kate for leaning out the window for a better view of the manscape. The nasty fall that follows isn't part of her fantasy—but the man who saves her from splattering the sidewalk is definitely the star.

When Mike personally attends to her injuries, she realizes her white knight in a hard hat has a tender side, giving her no choice but to surrender to the lust that's been arcing between them since day one. In the aftermath of the best sex of her life, she whispers her most secret desire: to be ravaged by his crew.

She never expected Mike would dare her to take what she wants—or that the freedom to make her most decadent desires come true could be the foundation for something lasting...

Warning: This book may cause you to spontaneously combust as five hot guys bring a woman's wildest fantasies to life during one blazing summer affair.

Excerpt From Kate's Crew:

Kate wiped her palms on her paint-splattered cutoffs before adjusting her grip on the rebuilt window casement. A flash of tan skin drew her attention to glistening muscles. They rippled over five sexy frames as the crew renovating the townhouse next door hammered nail after nail into their first-story roof, just a few feet below her perch.

From inside the bedroom where she worked, she inched to the edge of the ladder rung then craned her neck through the opening in front of her for a glimpse of the intricate tattoo spanning Mike's broad shoulders. Instead, she caught him reaching up to their stash of supplies for another pack of shingles. When her gaze latched onto the drop of sweat that slid along his neck, she forgot to breathe. She watched in fascination as it journeyed over his defined pecs and six-pack abs. After it was absorbed in the ultra-low-riding jeans snugged to his trim hips by a bulging tool belt, she heaved a sigh of relief.

Kate swiped at a blob of paint that had plopped onto her wrist unnoticed while she'd ogled Mike. Her tongue moistened her lips as she imagined licking a similar trail down his body. The edge of the fresh trim gouged her thigh as she strained for a better view. The gasp she made busted her. His head lifted, catching her spying. Great, now she'd never convince him to take it easy with his persistent innuendo or date invites. And, no matter how much she wanted to, she couldn't indulge either of their desires.

Mike threw her a dazzling victory grin. The anticipation sparkling in his cocky stare blasted a shockwave through her, screwing with her balance. The ladder wobbled then tipped. She probably could have righted herself if she hadn't been standing on tiptoes to maximize her view of the scenery. In slow motion, she watched his expression morph from flirtatious to horrified.

Kate flung out her arms in an attempt to catch the frame before she tumbled through it but the momentum swung her around. Her temple grazed the custom-made pewter latch she'd installed the day before. She hung, suspended in midair, as Mike rose from his crouch. The other guys began to turn toward her, but he was already sprinting for the edge.

Terror froze her insides when he launched himself across the ten-foot gap between their houses. Then she spun away, losing sight of him. She braced for imminent impact.

Shit, this is going to hurt.

Everything happened at once. Air whooshed from her lungs when she slammed, on her side, onto the roof. She rolled, flexing her ankles in an attempt to find purchase that would halt her skid toward the brink. But her knee wrenched at an awkward angle while she continued to rake over the slate. Her hand caught the ridge of an attic vent, slowing her descent, but gravity overcame the tenuous hold. Her frantic fingers recoiled from the sharp metal edge.

The gutters rushed closer, her last hope. After that, she'd have to pray the evergreen shrubs would cushion her, preventing any broken bones. The heels of her work boots hit the aluminum edging but kept going. Her legs dangled in thin air.

Then a strong hand banded around her wrist. Her arm nearly jerked from the socket as she lurched to a stop. Kate shoved on the edging shingles with her free hand, fighting to stay on the roof.

"Son of a bitch!" Mike hauled her the rest of the way up.

To keep reading Kate's Crew, click here.

NAUGHTY NEWS

Want to win cool stuff? Get sneak peeks of upcoming books? How about being the first to know what's in the pipeline or where Jayne will be making appearances near you? If any of that stuff sounds good then sign up for Jayne's newsletter, the Naughty News. She never shares you information, pinky swear!

www.jaynerylon.com/newsletter

WHAT WAS YOUR FAVORITE PART?

Did you enjoy this book? If so, please leave a review and tell your friends about it. Word of mouth and online reviews are immensely helpful and greatly appreciated.

JAYNE'S SHOP

Check out Jayne's online shop for autographed print books, direct download ebooks, reading-themed apparel up to size 5XL, mugs, tote bags, notebooks, Mr. Rylon's wood (you'll have to see it for yourself!) and more.
www.jaynerylon.com/shop

LISTEN UP!

The majority of Jayne's books are also available in audio format on Audible, Amazon and iTunes.

ABOUT THE AUTHORS

Jayne Rylon is a New York Times and USA Today bestselling author. She received the 2011 Romantic Times Reviewers' Choice Award for Best Indie Erotic Romance. Her stories used to begin as daydreams in seemingly endless business meetings, but now she is a full time author, who employs the skills she learned from her straight-laced corporate existence in the business of writing. She lives in Ohio with two cats and her husband, the infamous Mr. Rylon. When she can escape her purple office, she loves to travel the world, avoid speeding tickets in her beloved Sky, and–of course–read.

Opal Carew is the author of over a dozen romance stories in which she makes offerings of hope, success, and love to her readers. Opal loves crystals, dragons, feathers, cats, pink hair, the occult, Manga artwork, and all that glitters. She earned a degree in Mathematics from the University of Waterloo, and spent 15 years as a software analyst before turning to her passions as a writer. Opal lives with her husband and two teen-aged sons in Ontario, Canada

New York Times and USA Today bestselling author Avery Aster pens The Manhattanites, a contemporary erotic romance series of full-length, stand-alone novels, and the naughty new adult prequel companion series The Undergrad Years. As a resident of New York City and a graduate from New York University, Avery gives readers an inside look at the city's glitzy nightlife, socialite sexcapades and tall tales of the über-rich and ultra-famous.

Jayne Loves To Hear From Readers

www.jaynerylon.com
contact@jaynerylon.com

ALSO BY JAYNE RYLON

Nailed to the Wall

Hammer it Home

HOT RODS

Powertools Spin Off. Keep up with the Crew plus...

Seven Guys & One Girl. Enough Said?

King Cobra

Mustang Sally

Super Nova

Rebel on the Run

Swinger Style

Barracuda's Heart

Touch of Amber

Long Time Coming

STANDALONE

Menage

Middleman

4-Ever Theirs

Nice & Naughty

Contemporary

Where There's Smoke

Report For Booty

COMPASS BROTHERS

Modern Western Family Drama Plus Lots Of Steamy Sex

Northern Exposure

Southern Comfort

Eastern Ambitions

Western Ties

COMPASS GIRLS

Daughters Of The Compass Brothers Drive Their Dads Crazy And Fall In Love

Winter's Thaw

Hope Springs

Summer Fling

Falling Softly

PLAY DOCTOR

Naughty Sexual Psychology Experiments Anyone?

Dream Machine

Healing Touch

RED LIGHT

A Hooker Who Loves Her Job

Complete Red Light Series Boxset

FREE - Through My Window - FREE

Star

Can't Buy Love

Free For All

PICK YOUR PLEASURES

Choose Your Own Adventure Romances!

Pick Your Pleasure

Pick Your Pleasure 2

RACING FOR LOVE

MMF Menages With Race-Car Driver Heroes

Complete Series Boxset

Driven

Shifting Gears

PARANORMALS

Vampires, Witches, And A Man Trapped In A Painting

Paranormal Double Pack Boxset

Picture Perfect

Reborn

Made in the USA
Middletown, DE
15 October 2023

40808217R00080